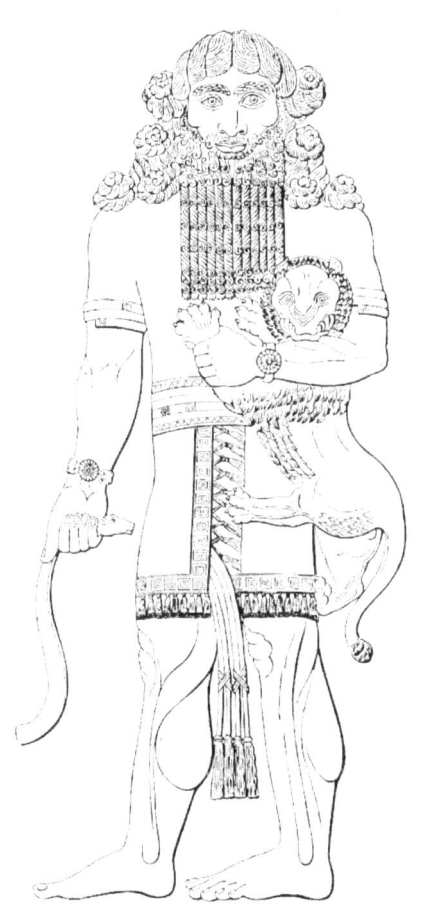

DEEP OVERSTOCK

#24: Classics
May 2024

❝ A classic is a book that has never finished **❞**
saying what it has to say.

Italo Calvino

CLSCS - CLASSICS

Editorial

EDITORS-IN-CHIEF: Mickey Collins & Robert Eversmann

CLASSICS EDITOR: Heather Hambley

MANAGING EDITOR: Z.B. Wagman

POETRY: Timothy Arliss OBrien, Jihye Shin & Nicholas Yandell

PROSE: Robert Eversmann

ADDITIONAL COPYEDITING: Simone Bouchey

COVER: "Hercules & the old man of the sea" New York Public Library Digital Collections.

CONTACT: editors@deepoverstock.com
deepoverstock.com

On the Shelves

7   alexander grooming by Aletha Irby

8   Advice on a Grecian Beach by Marianne Taylor

9   Let Us Be the Steward of Hamlet by Lynette Esposito

11   The Pyramids by John Delaney

12   The Graduate Library by Craig Sautter

34   Medusa by Marianne Taylor

35   THE LADY OF THE RIVER by Geoffrey Heptonstall

36   SCHEHERAZADE BIDS GOODNIGHT TO HER DOORKNOB by RJ Equality Ingram

37   Mr. Sammler's Planet by Michael Loyd Gray

39   Burned Child by Marianne Taylor

40   A Souvenir of Sand by John Delaney

42   Stonewalling by Ken Gosse

43   Camelot by Janis Lee Scott

46   Galehaut & Lancelot: A futuristic retelling of Arthurian legend by Nicholas Yandell

56   SCHEHERAZADE BIDS GOODNIGHT TO HER SISTER by RJ Equality Ingram

57   THE SEAFARER by Geoffrey Heptonstall

58   The Marble Halls of Arts & Letters - book 1 by Timothy Arliss OBrien

73   Van Gogh's Night by Lynette Esposito

74   To William Wordsworth by James B. Nicola

75   At the State Fair by Marianne Taylor

76   Henna by John Delaney

78   First of the Slut-Shamed: A Hymn for Helen of Troy by Ivy Jong

81   town crier by Aletha Irby

82   Bluebeard's Greatest Lie: A Creative Latin Composition Inspired by Carmen Maria Machado's In the Dream House by Heather Hambley

85   SCHEHERAZADE BIDS GOODNIGHT TO HER SONS by RJ Equality Ingram

86   To Have and To Hold by Miles Kenny

Continued...

91 Girls in Winter Triptych by Kate Falvey

93 MEASURE RESTORED by Geoffrey Heptonstall

94 Eadweard Muybridge Time 11-15 by Christopher Barnes

96 The Minor Keys by David de Young

97 Fourteen by Ten (a Sowhynot) by Ken Gosse

98 Buying a Leather Jacket in Fez by John Delaney

100 A Doorway by Marianne Taylor

102 Les Misérables Reviewed by Lynette Esposito

103 Dancing Cherubs, Hotel de la Marine, Paris 1° by Roger Camp

Letter from the Editors

Dearest Readers,

Stories have been around as long as humankind could speak and could ask about your weekend. Most of these stories have been lost to the ages of time and the hubub of the watercooler, but those that are still read and talked about hundreds and thousands of years after being thought of are truly classics. But Classic stories with a capital C are more than just an English class assignment.

What makes a Classic classic is up for debate. Generally, they are stories that have stood the test of time and have created an impact on culture. Calling something a modern classic is a bit of an oxymoron, because how can anyone know that something today will be considered a classic in the future? And yet here in your hands you hold a modern classic with *Deep Overstock 24: Classics*.

With riffs and commentaries on Classics that have come before as well as new poems and short stories which will shortly become classics in their own right, this is a *Deep Overstock* for the ages. These are the new literary crop that will one day sit among the greats, in our humble opinion.

As this issue come to a close, we shun the past and ask you for submissions in a totally different reality or future with our next issue: *Sci-Fi/Fantasy*.

Yours, tried-and-true,

Deep Overstock Editors

alexander grooming
by Aletha Irby

a masculine marmalade
our feline bathes
between his toes
more assiduously
than anyone we know
claws flexing
to and fro
like translucent crescent moons
cored by conquered blood
the rasping stroke
of his scouring tongue
a ferocity pristine
as raindrops or water hose
among the wielded
yielding thorns
of this bucephalus-headed rose.

Advice on a Grecian Beach
by Marianne Taylor

*"...She cannot fade, though thou hast not thy bliss,
Forever wilt thou love, and she be fair!"*
                    John Keats, "Ode on a Grecian Urn"

Don't let him take those pictures

when the water melts
luminous pearl around you
and the last sunbathers

ascend the pale ribbon trail
leaving behind
the day's opalescent heart

when only your swimsuits
still sleep on sand
the color of new honey

Honey
no matter what he says

for ever on some dusty shelf
you'll lie, breasts gleaming
in light's last sheen

long after
beauty's untrue

Let Us Be the Steward of Hamlet
by Lynette Esposito

He was a son gone somewhat wrong
in his talking to ghosts and speaking
of dreams.
Since he is alone in his monologue,
we should join him on stage--
wrap our spindly arms around his Princely shoulders
and whisper *it will be all right.*
Even if we see death coming,
we can teach him to dodge.

The Pyramids
by John Delaney

In the sandy haze, the pyramids rise
like apparitions. There is nothing else
visible in this land of sand and rock
and rubble. They have spent a long time

acclimating to the harsh conditions.
It's hot and dry and gets unbearable,
but still they patiently impose their presence,
having prolonged the inevitable.

They challenge us to think big, to work hard
together, to take the long view.
They assume a kind of cheerleading role.
'You can do better. Make time count. Be true.'

When you stand close to the stone blocks
and touch their weathered skin, straining to see
the top, you wish your life could be
part of something as extraordinary.

The oldest of the Seven Wonders of the Ancient World, the Great Pyramid of Giza was built in the 26th century B.C., primarily of limestone. Granite blocks in the King's Chamber weigh up to 80 tons. The structure is approximately 2.5 football fields square, oriented to the four points of the compass, almost 500 feet high, and consists of more than 2 million large stone blocks.

The Graduate Library
by Craig Sautter

When I was a rather new student at the University where I first naively sought Enlightenment, a mere Idealist devoted to the pursuit of esoteric knowledge whose dimensions I could not remotely grasp, whose complexities I could only vaguely anticipate, whose truths I did not yet dare question, I devotedly spent long autumn evenings secluded in the Main Reading Room of the Graduate Library. Utterly impervious to the titillating pleasures discovered by my fellow students as they ambled across the campus hand-in-hand in pursuit of new love, I was engrossed in the impenetrable arguments of an obscure philosophical text. Oblivious to the red and yellow Beech and Elm, Gingko and Frangipani leaves of that fading season fluttering down from branches outside its gothic walls, I ponderously read the sacred document, word for word, line by line, over and over, futilely trying to comprehend its meaning. With my head reverently bowed and precariously supported by nearly numb arms planted on one of the many long polished teak tables of that enormous hall shielded by broad beams of its awe-inspiring cathedral ceiling, I pretentiously sought secrets that were oh so slow forthcoming. And for some unknown reason, I endured, week after week. Somehow, I had finagled a coveted pass to that sanctuary from a graduate assistant with whom I exchanged my dorm meal pass for a month, to eat instead at Scotty's, a cheap burger and dog stand downtown, while I still examined dense commentary on the philosopher's murky passages, before I returned to my reserved seat in that hallowed chamber.

One night deep into that semester, after long sequences of such meditation, I unconsciously looked up across the study table to encounter two intense black eyes staring at me with amused contempt. "Was I an itinerant trespasser, a homeless intellectual vagabond intruding where I did not belong, or just an innocent wayward fool of some kind?" they seemed to inquire. I stared back, blankly, for my eyes, yawning brown in sunlight, glowing hazel in the moonlight, were then reddened from the weariness of intense reading and took more than a moment to refocus on human shapes and their inquiries.

"Hello," he said, rather more friendly than I expected.

"Yes, hello," I answered uncertainly, not knowing what else to say.

"You seem rather serious for an undergraduate intruding into our sacred domain."

"Undergraduate? How do you know I am an undergraduate?"

He simply smiled. I later learned he knew every graduate student who used the library's resources, their assigned seats, and the topics of their investigations.

"Well, I find the seriousness here conducive to study."

"You know there is a rather good Undergraduate Library next door where I believe you actually belong. There's even a comfortable reading room on the top floor frequented by honor students."

"Yes, I know, but most students there seem more interested in each other than in the books they pretend to read. They spend their time whispering coquettishly to one another," I said defensively. "I like this solitude."

"True enough. But do you presume to some higher aspirations than general undergraduate comprehension?" he gently mocked.

"I suppose I do," I answered somewhat apprehensively, afraid that he was about to expose me to the literary authorities of the place, not knowing he was one of them.

"And what is that you are reading so intently, my friend?"

Was he interested or just ready to ridicule me? I hesitated, looked him over, tried to read his intentions. He had a head of cropped short blond hair with a premature trace of gray on each side, a broad clean face, sharp nose and chin that would have made him seem somewhat handsome, were it not for his hunched shoulders, curved spine, and awkwardly short arms. He gave off a monkish appearance of a sequestered scholar, quite out of place in a room full of young, well-dressed, and affluent graduate students in their tweed jackets, white blouses, and thin blue or pink V-neck sweaters. For that reason, I was indecisive, then realized I had no recourse except honesty.

"*Immanuel Kant, Critique of Pure Reason*," I mumbled, somewhat embarrassed by my obvious over-reach. I had spent hour upon hour, week on week, trying to decipher the structure of his "Transcendental Apperception" in an elusive attempt to trap the post-Aristotelian, non-Substantiality of the "Self" that he sought to prove stood unseen as synthesis behind all events we experience, but whose phantom presence forever seemed to escape me like shadows of memory projected on the dusted white screen of my personal history whenever I looked for it.

"Ah, I should've guessed, Philosophy, that absurd rabbit hole of intellectual futility," he laughed.

"I think it's more serious than that," I tried to rebut him in defense of my intended Major. I was only taking "Introduction to Philosophy," a large lecture class taught by an animated Medieval Scholar of some note. "At least I can't reach such a conclusion until I've given it much more study."

"Why start with one of the most difficult books?"

I said nothing. The truth was that I had heard of Kant and simply had seen the word "Reason" in his title and reasoned it must be important. I thought I could cut corners and get to the heart of the philosophical enterprise. After all, I had read some Plato and a little Aristotle in my high school Philosophy classes. I'd heard that Kant was pivotal. Why, I had not a clue, certainly knew little of the challenges to him via Descartes, Berkeley, or Hume who had awaken the august German thinker from his "dogmatic slumber."

"Suddenly mute? Indeed, you must be a misguided freshman."

I stared menacingly back at him without answering.

"In that case, you should know that you've barely begun to make your way through the '100s,'" he said enigmatically.

"Pardon?" I had no idea what he was talking about.

"The '100' section of the Dewey Decimal System around which the volumes of this library are organized."

"Well then, at least I've started near the beginning," I played along.

"You have a long way to go. You're actually only on the ground floor in the Reference Room, where there is a little of everything," he added. "Eight floors still to traverse. Can you make it in four years?"

"Probably not. But this is where they keep commentaries on Kant, in Reference. Maybe I'll just make it to the 200s. Who knows?"

"Ah, the 200s, that's Religion, Faith, the antithesis of Rationality. If you are headed that way, why waste your time here?" He had a way of challenging me that made me mad.

"The number system seems reversed," I retorted. "Religion should come first, at least chronologically. But Rationality supersedes Religion and seems to be the foundation of modern Civilization." I thought myself somewhat informed on the subject, a prima facie argument for my behavior.

"Says who?"

I hesitated. "Says all of Science, says the Law, says Higher Learning itself." I felt confident in my answer, at least at that moment.

"Perhaps you haven't noticed a glaring lack of Rationality in our current world affairs, not to mention the century of slaughter we have barely survived? Wither Rationality in time of war, which seems to be all of the time? Wither Rationality in recurring famine amidst our ungodly and selfish affluence? Wither Rationality amid the ceaseless waves of personal hatred and jealousy that turn Brother against Brother and Sister? Wither Rationality when Democracy promotes the mass Idiocy that seems to reign supreme across the political landscape? If you're not looking for religious awakening in the 200s, then you're better off headed for fiction or poetry in the upper levels. At least they have no pretention to salvation. They are hidden up on the eighth floor."

"Well, you're quite the cynic," I shot back. "Is Rationality not residing here, at least," I replied, "at the core of all these volumes?" I dramatically flailed my arms about in a circular direction at the glossy wooden shelves filled with books of all sizes, from all eras, covering all sorts of fields, volumes that I could never hope to read this year or all of my years in the University.

"Ah, a true devotee to the philosophical tradition. So you're going to stick with the 100s. Not a bad stab at your defense, though." He smiled. His lower teeth were somewhat crooked. "All right, you can stay for now. And perhaps if you behave yourself, sometime I will take you on a tour of the upper floors of the 'Stacks' so you can see how far you have to go to gain a well-rounded 'Liberal Education,' to be the 'Renaissance Man' you are aiming to become."

I later learned the "Stacks" were the countless rows of crowded bookshelves above the open first floor leading all the way up into the Clock Tower where the most valuable volumes of the University's "Rarest Book Collection" were protected. Only professors and select graduate students were allowed in the "Stacks." Normally, students were required to sit in the Reading Room and submit individual book requests by their "Call Letters" found in the Card Catalogue so librarians or other graduate employees could carefully retrieve them and bring them down for examination or check out.

"And who are you who would grant me such an honor?" I arrogantly asked. Was he toying with me, I wondered contemptuously.

"Roland Clovis, Assistant Graduate Humanities Librarian. And this is my domain. I'm the one who issues permission slips to sit here for novices such as you." He stuck out his short right arm with a chapped white hand. "With whom do I have the pleasure of scholarly combat?"

I introduced myself and confessed that indeed I was a wayward freshman. He grinned at my honesty, slowly turned, surveyed the room, and walked away with a slight limp to assume his watchdog position on a tall swivel seat behind a raised reference desk guarding the entrance to the "Stacks" and paid no more attention to me that evening, although he always politely nodded whenever I entered or withdrew from the Reading Room in weeks and months to come when I appeared after classes or dinner. The Reading Room was open until midnight, seven days a week, although on Sundays, it didn't open until one in the afternoon.

Autumn retreated to early winter. I took the Thanksgiving break to go home for the first time since late August and returned to the disturbing scene of prolonged battles between my newly-divorced parents who gathered once more, mostly for the sake of my younger high school sister, and to endure their cross-examinations as they sought to discover whether their hefty tuition money had been wasted, as they presumed it had been on my idle studies, rather than some boring commercial business or professional preparations. At least the turkey, mashed potatoes, and tender asparagus sprinkled with almonds were a genuine reprieve from the cardboard roast beef and tasteless oatmeal of my dorm cafeteria. Two days later, I returned to school on the same ten-year-old Greyhound that had ushered me home, to write a number of five-to-ten-page final term papers, take blue book exams, and watch my first semester end with a string of four "As," in Philosophy, World History, English, and Astronomy, and only one "B+," in badminton and bowling from the required Physical Education curriculum intended to make America's youth stronger and better prepared for what? The next war?

I figured I would avoid my parents' distress by skipping Christmas vacation at home and hid out for twelve vacation days in my deserted dormitory room, high up on the seventh floor, gazing out across the University and dull lights of the small college town when darkness fell after four each afternoon. Both libraries, Undergrad and Graduate, which I could see on the far side of the campus, were closed for the break. But I could hear the Graduate Library Clock Tower bell chime away each hour, a lovely sound, I thought back then.

    Christmas, of course, was a bleak affair, sleet and freezing rain, the ball fields of yellow grass fading from dirt brown to scattered white, the bare wet trees that lined fraternity row turned funeral black, no presents from Santa. Old Saint Nick must have figured the dorms were deserted. Nothing from my family, the dorm mailroom was closed. A present came when it opened up again in January. I gave my folks a morning call and told them I missed them, asked my sister about her boyfriend to embarrass her. My mother cried a little. I had never been away for Christmas. Fortunately, the dorm cafeteria was shut down too. I ate popcorn and coke for breakfast, took a long walk around campus, the gyms were closed so I couldn't play any ball, my other passion. I spent the afternoon reading a Greek History textbook for a class that I had signed up for second semester. (I had already given up on Kant on page 277 for a while.) I took a nap and then, after reading some local sports pages about the upcoming Bowl games, decided to venture downtown to find someplace open for a square Christmas dinner. At least I figured I'd get a good turkey sandwich.

    Darkness was closing in as I walked the mile across campus to the legendary Gables, the only close place open that holiday evening. The old soda shop where jazz great Bix Beiderbecke once played trumpet to Hoagy's ragtime piano back in the 1920s had become a bar and grill. Someone told me Hoagy wrote "Stardust" there. Could be. It was usually packed with drunken fraternity brothers and their sorority princesses. But the food was always good. That night it stood depressingly deserted since almost all the students were back home. I walked in anyway and took a table by the window where I could watch cold rain embroider the empty avenue with oily silver-blue stains sparkling under a foggy yellow streetlight. After I took off my leather high school letter jacket, I glanced over at the silent jukebox and decided to play "White Christmas" just for a joke. On the way back to my table, I walked past a row of mostly empty booths. Then I heard a sharp voice.

"Is that the wayward philosopher?"

I wheeled around. I already knew who it was before catching sight of him in the shadow of the last cubicle. "Mr. Clovis."

"Get your coat and join me. Christmas is no time to eat alone."

I wasn't really in the mood for company but suspected loneliness was a terrible disease, and he evidently was suffering from it, as was I. "Sure."

I can't remember what we talked about at first, lots of shallow humor and witticisms, no doubt about holiday cheer and White Christmases. He insisted I buy more than a sandwich and graciously paid for my turkey and mashed potato dinner, with cranberries. He was drinking Irish whiskey with his meal. I thought of that old George Thorogood ballad, "When I drink alone, I prefer to drink by myself." Maybe not. They would have carded me if I had tried to order the same. Anyway, I'd had a couple of beers back in the dorm. I do remember the conversation slowly took a more serious tone. He cross-examined me about my background, my family, my friends, my goals in and after school, why I wasn't home for Christmas. I was as vague as I could be, for a while.

Eventually, his interrogation broke me down. I confessed to my isolation, admitted that I was indeed too serious for my own good. And under his further psychological probing, I admitted to trying to escape the rituals of first-year social initiations, that is, that I was too shy to try my luck with any of the pretty young co-eds who glided about campus. And there were plenty of them. I kind of resented his persistence and at some point even wondered if he was trying to pick me up or something, especially after he revealed some of his own vulnerabilities, something I didn't expect, and at first, wasn't all that eager to hear about. It was my own fault. I tried to deflect his questions with my own.

"What about you?" I'd finally got the courage to ask.

He hesitated. Faculty and staff aren't supposed to reveal too much about themselves, especially to undergrads. But he'd had two whiskies while we sat together, and probably at least a couple before I got there. He said he'd been on campus for almost two decades, was a kind of exile from his ecclesiastic aspirations. "I spent my high school and early college years in a Monastery down South, miles from nowhere." I detected slight traces of a Southern accent.

I found out he'd been a brilliant but errant student under the strict disciplinary routine of austere Monastic authorities. "They tried to teach me obedience by sticking me with mundane and meaningless tasks such as peeling potatoes, washing stacks of dishes, cleaning their small rooms, and damn toilets, before I was allowed to return to the consolation of my reading and prayers each evening. I hated some of them who tormented me, especially Brother Mathias." He took another drink.

It turned out he had an almost photographic memory and had memorized much of the Bible by the time he was through with his high school routine, and Brother Mathias, a sadistic pedantic, and perhaps pederast, I guessed, resented that more than anything. But to Brother Martin, the elder cleric, Clovis was a prized young scholar who could bring distinction to their Order. Brother Martin gave him free reign of their small library of sacred texts, many of its volumes in Latin, which by his last year there Clovis knew fluently, along with Greek and German. Unfortunately for him and his hopes for the priesthood, he stumbled upon a forgotten Latin volume by the Roman poet Lucretius, hidden on a top shelf of the library, stuffed in a mislabeled box.

"*De Rerum Natura*, 'The Nature of Things.' Have you read it?"

I said I'd heard of it in my high school Philosophy class. That was about it.

"Lucretius was an admirer of Epicurus, the Greek contemporary and opponent of Socrates and Plato. Unlike Plato, an Idealist who posited a theory of Absolute Ideas for the Forms of 'The Good, The True, and The Beautiful' in a higher reality, Epicurus was a radical Materialist who reduced everything to Matter in motion. And, as far as the Church was concerned, Epicurus was an enemy of all religions." Clovis rattled off a line of Lucretius in Latin, then translated for me, "Humanity is crushed under the weight of Religion."

I kind of agreed. "Heavy. When did he write that?"

"First century B.C. *De Rerum Natura* was an explanation of how everything that exists is ordered matter, not by the gods and their generosity or vengeance, but through the random combination of tiny, invisible Atoms, and that over an Infinity of events, all things are created and destroyed, time and time again."

"Wow. He knew about Atoms. When was that?" I was impressed.

"Before the reign of Christ. Amazing isn't it? But it was theory, not empirical science," which came sixteen centuries later.

"Still, pretty astute."

"Lucretius wrote that all religions seek to manipulate and terrify us with fear of punishment in some nebulous afterlife, but that in truth, we have nothing to fear from the gods, because they don't exist, and that we should seek tranquility and resignation in the impersonal laws of nature, of which we are a part and always will be."

I was enthralled by his Latin quotations, and intrigued how it all affected him. "When I read the lines of Lucretius, I instantly saw how everything I had previously been taught and believed was the result of Divine Design, could better be explained by dispassionate physics. Epicurus and his Atoms created the intellectual framework for modern science, for what we call scientific knowledge!"

I nodded and listened carefully. I knew I'd have to read Lucretius for myself.

"I saw the Light," he shook his head. "But it was not the Sacred Light that struck down Saint Paul on the road to Damascus. Epicurus and his Atoms provided a more compelling and obvious account for the universe than some invisible religious Spirit or the Holy Trinity that had shaped my life up until then. I yielded to Ockham's Razor, the simplest explanation."

He called for another whiskey, then fell silent for a moment. I ordered another Coke.

"That must not have gone over well with the Brothers," I half-joked.

"The text that I secretly translated from Latin in my small room when I was supposed to be engaged in prayer elevated the level of Doubt that I had hitherto repressed into utter defiance. I was ruined, even before my illicit literary excursions were discovered and deemed Heretical by my elders. I was denounced by Brother Mathias, who, suspecting something strange was going on with me, searched my room and found the volume behind my metal bed. He knew enough Latin to read the title and knew what it contained. He was both shocked and gleeful that I was guilty. So I was expelled from the Order that had guided my spiritual education for almost a decade. I was cast out like a venomous demon. I was only twenty-one."

All I could say was, "Gee, I'm sorry. That was cold." He downed his third or was it sixth glass. "Did you return home?" I asked.

He had no home. His father was in the military overseas. His mother had disappeared when he was young. In exile, he made his way to our University because he had a cousin in a sorority here, but she was about to graduate and leave him alone again. He stayed, worked weekends and summers for tuition, then got a scholarship. Within four years, he earned his Ph.D. in Greek and Latin Studies and in another two years in Religious History, plus an MS in Library Science in an additional year. For a while, he taught part-time in the Classics Department and lectured in Religious Studies. But tradition is that you move on to some other college to start your academic career.

"I didn't want to move on. I loved the serenity I found here, the beauty of the place. Luckily, I was offered a position on the University library staff, a non-academic appointment, and have worked my way up to Assistant Director of the Graduate Library's Humanities Collection, the closest thing I could find to a monastery."

At first, I thought his sad story made his apparent hostility toward Philosophy much more understandable, since it had ruined his life. But he wanted no pity, or so he said.

"I guess ultimately, it was for the best," he quietly claimed. "For here I am in what Leibniz ironically pronounced the 'Best of all Possible Worlds,' not the 'Real Secular World,' of course, but our 'Idealistic University World.' It is comfortable and enlightening. And I meet people I like, fellow seekers, so to speak." He smiled at me rather oddly. I guessed he was plenty drunk by then.

I nodded. I was a refugee myself, at least then, but I was caught off guard by his honesty and afraid that he wanted me to openly sympathize. I wasn't into sympathy back then, except for myself. He became quiet and that unnerved me. So I rather stupidly asked him if he had gone to Church that day. After all, it was Christmas and he had been raised in a Monastery.

He laughed softly and confessed, "Yes. I guess, ultimately, I still find more comfortable answers in Religion than Lucretius can give me, even if they are false. I'm not a scientist. Nor am I satisfied with his explanation of Spirit or Soul. They seem so different than mere Matter, even though they may have emerged from Matter. I'm a Dualist, Spirit and Matter. Plus, I came to see the tragic limits of 'Reason.' In the modern world, 'Reason' and science have fueled as much military destruction and human suffering as they have created invention and human comfort. Besides, it's hard to shed old habits. At least I'm not enslaved by the Priesthood. I am a free Spirit. All explanations are flimsy guesses."

I was surprised. I had been brought up Catholic, too. It haunted me sometimes. Yet I had fled from its dogmatic answers. That's why I was pursuing philosophy. I was, with Lucretius, a witness to endless creation and destruction of personal dreams and refused to give in to religious superstition or fear of damnation. Back then, I disdained Religion, at least Western Religion. Yet, in high school, I had been sort of enthralled by the Theosophists, Madame Blavatsky and all of her mysticism, which I later learned really came from the unified consciousness of self and Self in the Hindu *Upanishads*, and in America, by way of Emerson and the Transcendentalists. I was confused. Then I opted for Philosophy.

"What about you? Church on Christmas?" he asked hopefully.

"No, I gave up Church last Lent," I tried to joke. He didn't smile at that one. "Faith and Reason clash as far as I can see, and as I said the first time we met, I am a Rationalist, if not a Humanitarian or something. Still searching."

"Well, does Science subsume Religion, or Religion subsume Science? Anyway, keep searching," he advised. "I won't tell you what to believe. That's why you're here, to discover Truth for yourself." That was generous of him. I could see he was a good man, a learned man, a tormented man, but a kind man.

When we finished eating, he surprised me again with an invitation to walk two blocks over to the Graduate Library. "I have a key, of course, the key to knowledge," he chuckled as he limped up the hill on which the two libraries stood silhouetted against the raw night.

We approached the large, darkened limestone structure built back in the 1920s, its only illumination coming from the round white face of the large clock on its Romanesque tower. Almost ten o'clock, I remember it read. We'd been talking for several hours. The building's steep red-tiled roof glistened in a steady rain that was changing to light snow as it got colder. We entered through a back door used for deliveries. He punched a few numbers into the security alarm system, and we walked up the back steps and wound our way into the Main Reading Room that dimly glowed with a few low-power night lights. I had never seen it so dark or so completely deserted. It felt spooky, just the two of us, the empty tables, and thousands of books lining the walls, floor to ceiling. I thought maybe they were secretly communicating with one another in a silent language of the dark. I thought I could hear their wisdom bubbling up from the stillness. It was like we were disrupting a holy séance.

"Follow me. I'll show you the 'Stacks' and something even few Graduate students get to see." He pulled a flashlight from his coat pocket and we walked up another set of old wooden stairs behind the reference desk, stopping at each floor to note its contents while he uttered a few words of commentary. He told me there was a metal elevator for the book runners who retrieved the requested volumes, but this was the only way to reverently ascend through all the dimensions of human knowledge. I followed him without saying much.

The second floor contained the Philosophy section, the 100s that I read on the book bindings, a more complete collection than on the main floor of reference books. "Here's where I assume you'll waste most of your time these next few years," he humored me. "I recommend you start with Plato's *Republic*, rather than Kant." I didn't mention that I was scheduled to read it the next semester in my Political Theory class with Dr. Sorenson.

"'I walked down to Piraeus yesterday with Glaucon, son of Ariston, to make my prayers to the goddess.'" I looked at him inquisitively. "Plato's first line of the *Republic*, Socrates speaking," he told me. "Plato is setting up Socrates' inquiry into Justice in the State and in the Soul." I was flabbergasted. "Nowhere does that Dialogue tell the reader, and you must learn on your own, that Glaucon was Plato's older brother."

"Really!" I smiled in surprise.

And he did that with each book he touched during his

tour, scores of them, quoted lines that someday I would read on that night's recommendation.

"I guess you won't be too interested in the religious volumes on this floor, the 200s." I said nothing. We climbed another flight of stairs to the third floor and the 300s, Social Sciences. "*Democracy in America* by Tocqueville," he mumbled, "Veblen, Schlesinger, the Economics of Smith, Ricardo, Malthus, plus Education, Horace Mann, John Dewey and so forth." We passed through them as though they were nothing but popular prejudice, although he stopped here and there to quote. "Free public education is one of America's great gifts to the world," he asserted.

"Then how come I have to pay so much tuition?"

"Good question."

On the fourth floor, we quickly walked among the 500s, Mathematics, Euclid, Archimedes, Bertrand Russell and Whitehead's *Principia Mathematica*, the Pure Sciences, volumes on animals, badgers, wolves. He stopped to pull Ridgway's *Ornithology of Illinois*. "This is worth an afternoon or more up here," he commented. He pointed out the 600s, Medicine, Health, Technology. "The Technocrats," he said with a sneer, "one day they will run everything, and know nothing."

We ascended to the fifth floor, Arts & Recreation, oversized books on painting, photography, music. I caught sight of some titles in the shadows, Greek sculpture, Michelangelo, Rembrandt, Van Gough, Picasso, Warhol. I wanted to stop, look, listen to what he might say, but he pushed on past some Library offices.

The staircase became narrower as we approached the sixth floor "Stacks," the 800s, Literature. Here we stopped for more than half an hour while his hands, whitened from all the bleach he had been forced to use for cleaning toilets in the monastery, glided over the essays of Thomas Merton, who he knew by heart. "Art enables us to find ourselves and lose ourselves at the same time." He smiled. "Love is our true destiny.... We do not find the meaning of life by ourselves alone - we find it with another." He looked at me again and smiled. I felt uneasy. Then he passed on to Emerson, "Be yourself; no base imitator of another, but your best self…" He turned to me. "Good advice, no, even from a Philosopher?" Then he pulled out a volume by Proust, "Let us be grateful to people who make us happy; they are the charming gardeners who make our souls blossom." Then Balzac, "Love is the poetry of the senses." And Flaubert, "The art of writing is the art of discovering what you believe." He knew by heart all those French Masters, names I only vaguely heard of in high school, but one day would cherish.

    He led me by the sleeve, over to the long shelves of English, American, French, Russian, Iranian Poetry. His hands caressed the outer bindings as he repeated their names, Shakespeare, Milton, Robert Herrick, quoting wildly, drunkenly, as he limped forward. Finally, he stopped at Omar Khayyam's *Rubaiyat*, Fitzgerald's translation, and pulled it from the shelf. "At least you've heard of this one?" he chided me.

    I nodded. "Yes."

    Without cracking the cover he said, "I know it is only December, but listen to the wisdom of the poet. 'Come, fill the Cup, and in the fire of Spring, Your Winter garment of repentance fling, for the bird of Time has but a little way to flutter, And the Bird is on the Wing.'" I'd heard of the poem before in high school, but had never heard its verses recited so lovingly. I can never forget that stanza, as I hear it now in the echo of his voice.

    "We could spend all night here, but 'the bird is on the wing,'" he pushed the volume back into its snug sleeping place on the tightly packed shelf. I saw why they call them the "Stacks." We ascended to the seventh floor, History, the 900s. That's where I expected he would tell me something about the civilizations that rose long before ours, perhaps along the Indus River so he could lecture me on the Vedas or maybe retell a legend from Ur. But, no, we walked past old paper-bound accounts of our State when it was still Indian Territory, past the Congressional Records going back into the early 1800s, past the biographies of U.S. Presidents, the personal papers of Adams to Roosevelt, a shelf devoted to Lincoln.

We passed the volumes on Russian and European wars and empires until we reached the rear wall of the seventh floor and a locked door. He removed a skeleton key from his pocket key ring stuffed in his brown corduroy pants and opened it to reveal another set of steeper, narrower wooden stairs that led up into the Clock Tower room. He pushed aside some low-hanging, bare electric wires with a volume of Tolstoy in his hand. They gave off a spark and I jumped. "Careful! Don't touch them. They are dangerous hanging down like this. But paper doesn't conduct electricity." He tapped Tolstoy. "The University is going to renovate and rewire the entire library this summer. The building could be closed for three months. I don't even know if librarians will be able to get in. I may go to Europe, Rome, of course." I ducked and avoided electrocution. We ascended the last few stairs.

"This is what I wanted to show you." We had arrived at the end of the stairs, where he opened another gray metal door that led into a small room in the tower, carpeted with thick, old, and worn Oriental rugs, a heavy, brown, cracking leather couch, and two green, stuffed leather chairs. A couple of 1930s oil paintings of the nearby National Forest, streams, and fields filled with sunflowers were squeezed between floor-to-ceiling shelves. The back side of the tower clock lit up one side of the room. I could read 11:35 backward on the dial.

He turned on a green shade lamp. Then he went over to the fireplace and flipped a switch. Artificial flames flickered over fake logs, and then a spark surged up on the thin, bare wire behind. The lights dimmed for almost half a minute, and then the flames resumed. "Once this was a real fireplace, but that was too dangerous. They got rid of it in the 40s. Still original wiring, but it gives off the appearance of fire and actual heat. On cold winter nights, this is the best place on campus to read. Those wires are a problem they'll fix this summer."

"Cozy," I agreed.

"Yes. This is the Rare Rare Book Room, the public Rare

Book Room is in the back of the first floor. You've seen it. This one contains volumes of which there might be only a handful of copies in the entire world. Only the veteran librarians are allowed here and a few senior scholars and professors. I spend a lot of time in this room. Sometimes I even sleep on that couch." I was more than impressed as I followed behind him while he pointed out three display cases.

"Here's one of the original State Charters of 1816," he gestured. I looked closely at the ornate ink handwriting and the official State Seal. "Here's a copy of one of the first French maps of the Mississippi River, 1671." It was amazing how inaccurate it seemed. "And this is an original copy of Tom Paine's 'The Rights of Man,' 1791."

"Amazing." Of course, I was dazzled, almost speechless.

"They should be under lock and key, but so few people know of them up here. They've been safe this long." He jingled the keys in his pocket.

I pretended to zip my lips.

It was plenty warm up there. I was tired. I examined the books on the old shelves while he walked over to a desk and removed a half-finished bottle of Chivas Regal 25 from the bottom drawer. "How about a Christmas drink with me?"

My father kept good whiskey around the house, so I knew what he had. "Why not?"

"To friendship," he toasted.

"To knowledge," I replied.

His eyes were bloodshot and his speech slightly slurred. I felt a little uneasy drinking with University staff. But he wasn't Faculty, so I figured the rules might be a little different.

"Sit down," he pointed to the couch. I did. He downed another glass and then put the bottle back before he walked over to the far wall and pulled down a small metal box from the top shelf. "This is what I want to show you." He opened the container and removed a yellowed book with a faded paper cover. The title was in a hand scroll, written in Latin, *De Rerum Natura*.

"That's it?" I managed to gasp.

"Yes. I guess I should give you the real story. After Brother Mathias took it from me and told me he was going to burn it, he left it in his room and went to report me to Brother Martin. I broke in, stole it back, and fled the monastery. They expelled me when they discovered what I had done. But I was already gone. They ordered the local police to search the bus station and arrest me. But I had hitchhiked out of the county headed north. Eventually, they found out where I had landed, and they sued to get it back. But I had crossed state lines, and I hid it in a safe deposit box in a bank in the next county for a couple of years. They couldn't trace it and eventually gave up. I hid it in this rare book collection five years ago. I found out the details of what happened at the monastery after I left. At an academic conference in New York, I ran into a former fellow student who graduated the following year. He'd become a professor of History at Yale. I told him that they had lied, that Brother Mathias actually had burned it and that's why I fled. I think he believed my lie."

Clovis sat down beside me and ran his small fingers through its brittle pages. He halted, closed his eyes. I thought he had blacked out. Then he opened them and read a passage in Latin, and translated. He went on for a long time, and it was getting late, and I was becoming drowsy. I remember, his voice changed, became deeper and quavered as he quoted Lucretius. "It's easier to avoid the snares of love than to escape once you are in that net whose cords and knots are strong; but even so, enmeshed, entangled, you can still get out unless, poor fool, you stand in your own way." He smiled at me and asked, "Isn't that profound and lovely? Am I standing in my own way?"

I didn't reply.

"I've never really shared this volume with anyone before. It's been such a lonely journey for me." His voice cracked.

Things were so much different back then. A deep kind of

fear separated different kinds of people from each other in all sorts of ways; blacks from whites, white from blacks, men from women, boys from girls, young men from older men. And at that age, what did I know about the deeper mysteries of existence? I was just finding out. Some people hated others for who they were what they were. I never hated anyone. But I was no saint either. Sometimes I was often thoughtless and thus cruel when I never meant to be.

He put down his beloved Lucretius on the couch on his other side, the ragged text he had saved from the flames of the fearful Monks. Tears shaded his eyes. He looked at me for a long moment. He was so drunk. He closed his eyes again. I held my breath. When he opened them, he looked at me again, then put his hand on my knee.

I couldn't believe what was happening. I froze. I didn't know what to say. Fear shot through me like an electric circuit surging through bare wires. I knew I liked girls. I had a girlfriend at home, a pretty girl and smart, two years younger, or I had before I left for school and she started dating someone else, some footballer. I was so confused. I admired Mr. Clovis, I really did. I had found him fascinating, an intellectual hero, really. But that was all. That was plenty. But not enough. I leaped up.

"I'm really tired. I think I'm almost drunk. I'm sorry. I got to go. I got to go." I didn't even look at him. I just bolted through the door, rushed down the steps, across the seventh floor "Stacks," and then down the creaking wooden staircase we had climbed, floor by floor, into the basement and out the delivery door where we had entered. I heard an alarm go on, then shut off when I slammed the door. I didn't look back except once. I saw the light of the Clock Tower, 12:37. I walked rapidly, then ran for a while, exhausted, moved away as fast as I could the rest of the way back across campus now white in the day after Christmas snow.

Who was I running from? He couldn't have been behind me. I took the elevator up to my dorm room, locked the door, and sat in the dark. "Why did I act like that?" I asked myself over and over. "Why did I have to insult him that way? I could have just said, 'That's not my thing.' And after he'd gone out of his way to be so good to me? To try to help me. Or was he just setting me up the whole time? What will I say when I run into him again?"

I kept cross-examining myself, drank two beers, opened the window to let in some cooler air as I watched the snow swirl, and lay down on my narrow bed. I listened to the Library tower bell finally strike two. I thought I almost fell to sleep, shallow, restless sleep.

Then I heard it, a dull subconscious sound at first, and then it became a distant alarm. I thought I heard sirens. Half awake, I stumbled to my window overlooking the campus. The sirens became louder. Fire engine sirens. I looked across the campus toward the Graduate Library and saw small flames jetting up through the red-tiled roof. A horror gripped me. I jammed on my gym shoes as fast as I could, grabbed my coat, and ran, and ran, and ran, slipping on the snow, falling, getting up, running. The sirens screeched louder and louder the closer I got. I swept through the woods in the center of campus and came out on the other side to see the entire top floors of the Graduate Library consumed by flames.

"He's up there, help him, help him," I screamed at the first fireman I saw. "He's up there in the Clock Tower room. You've got to save him."

"Who is?"

"The librarian, Mr. Clovis. You've got to save him. He sleeps in the tower room." I was crying, screaming hysterically.

"God help him if he's up there now. Maybe he got down. Get back. I'll tell the Chief."

Just then the large white scorched face of the clock tumbled out of the tower and crashed to the ground leaving an ugly round hole in the upper wall. The tall Romanesque tower was crumbling, leaning to one side. Then I saw him, standing in the opening where the clock had been, his arms spread out, his clothes and hair on fire, but not a sound from him, like a martyr at the stake. Could he have seen me? He couldn't have. But I felt he had. I knew he had. He was holding something stretched out in his right hand. I heard a loud crack. The tower floor beneath him gave way, but as he fell back into the flames, he tossed it from the gaping hole where the clock had been. A light wind fanned its flames as it fluttered to the ground. I broke through the police line that was keeping the small crowd that had gathered away from the firemen. The book was all flames as it hit the snowy ground. I stomped on the half-burned volume of Lucretius, fell to my knees, picked up the crumbling hot pages. They burned my hands. I pressed the singed volume to my chest against my coat to smother the remaining fire. More than half of it was gone. He was gone. He was gone. And I knew somehow I was responsible.

"Damn wiring, it's ancient," I heard the Fire Chief swear to one of the police officers. "We gave them an order to fix it last summer, but they appealed and put it off a year. That's what it had to be, God Damn wiring."

"Yea. what the hell good did all that book learning do for 'em?" the cop muttered.

Medusa
by Marianne Taylor

Mostly my neck
just always hurts
they're heavy
never still or asleep at once
I rarely sleep myself

I feed them cat food
sometimes mice
the pet store girl is kind
looks at our shadow
wants to know their names
that they smell dead
when frightened
defecate in my brain
causing dark thoughts
My children were taken
I've never mothered
don't remember my own
trauma interferes they say
she who did this—her I recall
her volatile face
writhing in hate
over a god I didn't love
who smelled like fish and wrack
I've tried dating
those forms are awkward
no place to click "monster"
but I met someone anyway
and it's okay--they're blind
I'm used to being unseen

They want to paint my portrait
this might be exploitation
still, the scent of paint will be nice
and they'll have to touch me

What do you think will happen
when others see the work?

THE LADY OF THE RIVER
by Geoffrey Heptonstall

An Evocation of the T'Ang Dynasty

The leaves have fallen early this year.
Butterflies are pale and move slowly now.
The reeds reflect the water,
a blue shade neither sea nor sky.
The wind from the east brings rain
in clouds covering the whole earth.
At the water's edge the willows lament
the passing of the seasons
from heat to frost to snow,
a change like a lady's moods.
Her eyes are the phases of the moon,
her tears the petals of spring blossom,
her smile the grace of the mountain hare.
Where she walks the river flows freely.
The waters will rise in a flood
spilling onto the street beneath her window.
Her silken innocence flows on the high tide
as far as the bridge into heaven.

SCHEHERAZADE BIDS GOODNIGHT TO HER DOORKNOB
by RJ Equality Ingram

Little brass welt how dare you try to mock me
We've come farther in one thousand & one
Nights than any blue-eyed continental explorer
I should shove you in a junk drawer & lose you
For letting in the nameless men of the palace
Who have become accustomed to measuring
This cursed room for their next virgin prisoner
For years they never even unpacked my bags
I can't blame them when it's my guilty husband
Who ties us all around you w/invisible thread
But the truth is that I know you're needed here
If it wasn't me it'd be another soul to guard
Even if only for one last quiet cloudless night
I could swallow every key & still they'd find me

Mr. Sammler's Planet
by Michael Loyd Gray

There was an old woman. I was quite young and green to the ways of the world. She looked like she might be a homeless person wandering about the mall in her shabby topcoat and unkept, mop-like gray hair. But she wanted to read something serious, she said, and this was in my bookstore clerk days, long before I managed to climb an ivy tower and teach eager acolytes and write books that appeared in stores.

I steered her away from Romance to Literary Fiction. She seemed cowed by the immense wall of novels by the greats. She picked a book off the shelf – Dickens, maybe. Or Austen. I never really knew for sure. She held the book delicately, as though it burst into flames or just dissolve into dust in her hands.

She said she didn't know what was good and I admit that I had to suppress a smirk and turn my head to a side to hide what I have come to regret over the years: a casual sense of superiority – like that self-destructive fool Anders in the Tobias Wolff story.

Then the book appeared to grow heavy in her hand, and she shifted it to the other and back again, and I slipped it from her grasp and shelved it. She appeared relieved. Whichever great tome it was, it was certainly a heavy, thick book. Perhaps it was Pynchon, where literature is metered by the metric ton.

I judged (misjudged) her as paperback material, and so we strolled down the aisle, and I surveyed what we had: Hemingway and Fitzgerald and Faulkner and Flannery O'Connor and Eudora Welty, and all sorts of gems, but I didn't sense (arrogantly assumed) they were for her. I dared not toss the molasses of James Joyce at her.

She said she just wanted to pass the time. She thought reading was the way to go. I rubbed my chin absently with a thumb and surveyed the shelf. Looking back, I suspect it may have just been random, no real logic behind it: when I raised my hand to see what it held, I saw it was Saul Bellow's *Mr. Sammler's Planet*, and I handed it to her.

The paperback seemed the right weight for her, and she hefted it and smiled. She said she would take it but turned back on the way to the register and asked if it was any good. I told her it was absolutely superb, perhaps groundbreaking and all that. She frowned slightly and looked a little uneasy, but nodded and paid for the book.

That bookstore isn't even there anymore, all these decades later. I'm in another town, far away, at a blueblood university, my own books behind me on a shelf. I think of that woman and wish time was as malleable as Einstein suggested, and I could go back and apologize to her.

And I still have not read *Mr. Sammler's Planet*.

Burned Child
by Marianne Taylor

"At last a deed worth doing. I say there is beauty in this...."
                                                Henrik Ibsen, *Hedda Gabler*

Hedda, we misunderstood you,
saw a monster embodying
the Seven Deadlies,
a remorseless disrupter,
deceptive and cruel,
eluding boredom, inflicting
pain. But your handsome face
and warrior heart weren't
sensible gear for your day.

Were you a goddess, we'd expect
the flirting and grape leaves,
the manuscript burning impulse
at least. But the wheel dropped you
in the wrong era, in the midst of
those pistols, and the general
taught his daughter to shoot.

Shadow sister, feel our embrace
in your morbid parlor that reeks
of lavender and dried roses, know
that all these years later we still
question that beautiful bullet
in your temple. And some days
we seethe with your malice as well.

A Souvenir of Sand
by John Delaney

How to get familiar with infinity . . .
A camel ride into the Sahara
to stargaze a wide open desert sky?

The astronomer Carl Sagan once said
stars outnumbered grains of sand on beaches—
so I rode a camel from Merzouga

out into oceanic dunes of sand
and sat there after sunset for the stars,
dwelling for a time with two infinities,

it seemed, or was it two eternities?
I felt *forever* in the sandy dust
flowing like a fountain through my fingers.

I found endless sand and stars to ooh and ah.
Beholding leads to praying. Inshallah.

The Sahara's surface of sand measures approximately 3.5 million square miles, the size of the contiguous U.S. Washed by the wind rather than water, its fine grains are unsuitable for making concrete.

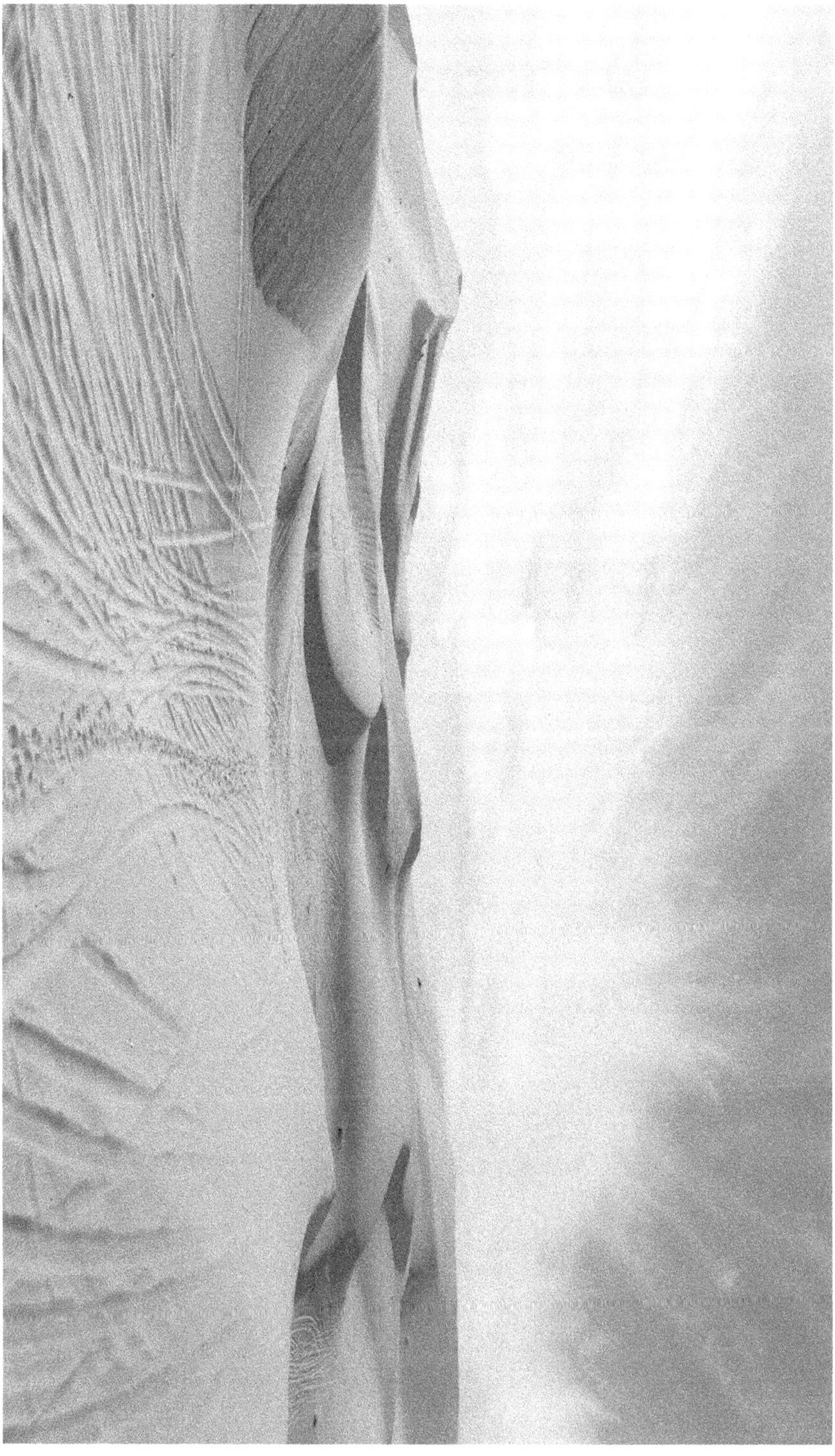

Stonewalling
by Ken Gosse

A Sonnet on Robert Frost's "Mending Wall"

Two neighbors both bring bricks in burly hands,
their gnarled knuckles ready for the task
of keeping neighbors friendly when demands
of conversation's more than they would ask.

They'll share a calloused smile once they've returned
each spring, to make sure neighbors will atone
with reparations for the damage earned,
effects of beasts and weather on each stone.

And then, the falsehood raised by hearty voice,
"Good fences make good neighbors!" Lovely wall,
beset with elves themselves who have no choice
but play their mischief, summer, winter, fall.

Returning home, as each walks back alone,
they'll wave a middle finger to the bone.

Camelot
by Janis Lee Scott

On November 22, 1963, Joan sat on the gym floor, dressed out for gym class when the news of President Kennedy's assassination blared through the loud speakers, reverberating down the halls.

Coach Mancini came out of the office to talk to her girls, tears streaming down her face. All stood as she gave the final report.

No one wanted to believe it. What if the news reports were wrong? Maybe he wasn't that badly hurt. Maybe someone else had been shot.

Mrs. Mancini took a deep breath in between all of the 'what-ifs' and began to sob. She suddenly shifted from her class, eyeing the comfort of her office, retreating and shutting the door.

Joan looked around the gym floor and spotted a wall free to sit. Her friends followed, mimicking her crossed-legged sit and dumb-stricken look.

Before hearing the news, basketballs had been checked out for shooting through the inside hoops. Now, Trudy and Ellen started dribbling the balls back to Joan and others, prompting a back and forth dribble. The balls made a hollow BOING sound. Joan thought of the week prior when students and faculty had been gliding across this waxed wooden floor for the monthly sock hop, gyrating to Elvis and Bill Hayley and his Comets. The sock hop had been exhilarating fun and now this doom, this hollow sound.

An early June evening found Joan and a couple of friends sitting at a dark, ornate table in the Exodus Library. Cyndee held up the long crumpled piece of paper Mr. Gardner had printed up. "He can't want us to go through this whole list for such a short 'fun' assignment?"

Joan shook her head no. "He wants us to choose a few reads about Merlin and King Arthur."

"Yeah, I think, he's trying to give us a break from the thirteen colonies." Loyal had already jumped up, grabbed the list out of Cyndee's hands, and headed for filing cabinets and correct rows.

"Here," Loyal said. "This'll cheer up your mood." He plopped "The Crystal Cave" in front of Joan on the dark table.

Cyndee popped her head up from her story. "Did Guinevere have any other lovers besides Sir Lancelot?"

Loyal gave Joan a you've-got-to-be kidding look before answering. "I don't think so."

Joan buried her head back in her book, feeling way to warm and comfy. She couldn't concentrate on what she read, dangerously close to falling asleep. She thought of the two men in dark suits, chasing her in so many dreams. She still didn't know why. Her mind wandered to soldiers in camouflage, searching for an enemy in darkness. She prayed they could stay safe.

Now, when Joan thought of Vietnam, she remembered President Kennedy's assassination. The two events had woven together in her memory like and intricate tapestry. She replayed the news clip in her head of Jackie reaching over the backseat of the convertible, trying to grab the secret service agent when the shots rang out. Jackie, stoic in the blood splattered pink suit, standing next to the Johnsons as Lyndon was sworn in as President on the Texas tarmac, waiting for the flight back to Andrews Air Force Base and Washington DC. Joan pictured John John as he saluted his father's coffin, proceeding toward its final resting place where the eternal flame burned.

Countless happier images rolled through Joan's brain: John John hiding under his father's desk in the Oval Office, Caroline steering her father's sailboat in Nantucket. "Camelot is really over," Joan whispered as the library closing lights flickered off and on.

"Lost in your thoughts, Joan?" Cyndee asked. "Did you say something?"

"No," Joan answered. "Not really."

Galehaut & Lancelot: A futuristic retelling of Arthurian legend
by Nicholas Yandell

Open your eyes.

Such a simple suggestion. From such roots of isolation, with so few options for self-determination, to now observe such spectacular transformation.

From a blur of a youth on a simple farm, in a place whose name I don't even know. To a family always called to duty, whose memory I barely hold. Left mostly alone in bunker schools, grasping at wood and stone, rubber and string, metals and plastics. I found in these materials such a fountain of prospects.

That first slingshot I made when I was maybe seven; it truly birthed something. After seeing a neighbor shoot a crabapple into a tree, I was mesmerized by the movements, and needed nothing more than memory to summon re-creation. I'd grasped not just structure but also purpose and motions, and after a week, and numerous prototype versions, I had created a slingshot surpassing my neighbor's in both distance and accuracy. And this led to such an avalanche of creativity, new devices with new intentions, and me, the happiest I'd ever been. All, of course, leading up to the explosion, on that returning ship, that took my parents to their graves.

Left too young for freedom, I scarcely survived in the crowded shelter. But when I received a cyber letter, with an envied key to the Industrial Army, even then I had my doubts. With my parents' service not forgotten, my coveted reward, a boarding school training program, with a spot for me. I had no real choice and was scared, but also intrigued, by what lay beyond the earth, the technologies and possibilities.

But the life I joined was anything but conducive to my impulsive creativity. It was forced isolation and rigged conformity, with rules that changed perpetually. Heights of competition, in a brutal game, with little option to depart our life-assigned lanes. I held out a desire to someday enter the creative sectors, but there were far too few fiercely protected positions and no one to take any interest in a farm boy, even one with inclinations towards invention.

Despite finding far too little meaning in the computations of their machines, I excelled and quickly climbed the ranks. With a flawless record, I not only passed with fluency all their computation and controller programs, but also became a skilled technician. Happily, that meant for me, solo missions with time during travel, to actually pursue my passions. Often I'd create new machines, and through long hours of testing volatilities, with a laser focus intensity, I'd breathe life into the calculated movements. Other times, I just lost myself in the joys of material combination, transcending any known purpose, but radiating aesthetic and emotional significance.

A life of precision, until I found myself on what was supposed to be a simple mission; one done numerous times before. Land robotic paladins in their pods. Clear out the destination. Hold the perimeter for the extractors to finish their duties. Everything to me was lights and shapes on a screen, and as long as the red circles stayed neutralized, my task was complete. I'd then depart the planet, and repeat the cycle, and never even step foot on the ground.

Until it all started that day with music, or that's what I thought. The degrading of what had become the mediative hums of my daily work. Interruptions of blips and bleeps and I had to dig deep, to remember in my training, what this could possibly be. Yellow lights, springing from square diagrams. Paladins were stalled, and likely from a bouncing red dot in close vicinity. At least all of it was isolated to a single spot on my little map screen.

Contacting my commander, I gave them an accurate description and transferred my readings, but there was still no clear cause and no managerial technician close enough to institute the necessary override. I was given clear instructions on how to approach the situation. Land a pod, and find a stalled paladin at a safe distance away from the perimeter actions. Diagnose problems, take images, and report back immediately. I was not to fix the problem, even if I could.

    This challenge was invigorating. The opportunity to actually walk on dirt again. Something I hadn't experienced since I'd left my childhood farm. Boarding my landing craft, equipped with a portable screen and paladin controls, I took off and landed safely within the established perimeter. Out of my craft, my feet hit the ground, and I could barely stand. Quickly though, it all came back, as I ran my gloved hand through the dirt, letting the grains waterfall through my fingers.

    I found nothing clearly wrong with the paladin. Some sort of glitch had left it dormant and resistant to my controls. I could easily have reset it, wiping all issues and sending it back to work, but that was not my instruction, so I simply wrote my report, and took the desired images.

    As my task was completed, I saw, deep in the distance, mysterious movement. As I matched it up to my screen, I noticed another yellow square appear, with a pulsing red dot striding away. I counted eight yellow symbols, and even though I controlled 500 paladins, continuing at this rate, this could really be a problem. I couldn't help but take a peek at the menace. With vision enhancing goggles, modified by me, I wouldn't even have to leave the spot I'd landed, and could still keep honest to my mission.

    When I zoomed in on the disturbance, it didn't make sense. A flash of skin amidst a mirrored glare. A male appearing person, with mostly bare skin, except for goggles, shoes, minimal waist covering, and a harness around his chest, attached to mechanisms that extended the length of his arms and up to his shoulders. His right hand held what appeared to be a mirrored shield, and his left, a mechanical pole with square objects on the end of it.

His movements though, were unlike those of any combatant I'd ever seen. More like those of a dancer than a soldier. With fluid agility, he deflected the paladin's beams with his shield, and then glided back and forth, slowly getting closer to it. Finally, he thrust out his pole and opened the objects on the end, just enough to clamp onto a spot in the upper middle of the paladin, which shook for a moment, and then stopped.

What was this guy doing? As tenacious as he was, he had to know that he couldn't possibly defeat this whole army. I knew he'd get tired and sloppy and get hit by a stray beam, and that'd be it for him. Still, he might take out a dozen more or so paladins before that happened. It was an urgent problem and I couldn't let it go. I'd worked too hard, for too long, to botch the first mission that required a planetary landing.

The guy was already working on number ten, when I took control of the paladin. Right as he got close, and began his pattern of attack, I changed the paladin's direction quite suddenly, and fired a laser at his feet. He nimbly leapt back just in time, but seemed quite shaken. That didn't last long though. He regrouped himself and came at my paladin once again. I fired at his chest, then quickly at his head, and he dodged one beam, and sent the other veering off with his shield. I gave him a rapid fire pattern of such extreme focus and agility, but he dodged it all. Not only that, he made an offensive move with his magnetic arm, and nearly struck my paladin, which I had to quickly throw into reverse.

Hours later, still a stalemate. Human determination unlike any ever seen. I was the one who was wearing out, even though I was only moving my fingers. All until I noticed on my screen, a small dip behind him, collapsed not long ago, after being hit with laser beams. Our ground became a chess board and I saw his demise emerge. Step by step re-created, while he executed his agile game until finally one of his feet landed in a completely unexpected place. He collapsed backward, his shield falling away.

I immediately shot his weapons from him and the pole ripped the harness off, throwing him back and leaving his chest a trail of bloody welts. Clearly wounded, he still tried to escape, but his leg had no support, and he tumbled back into the hole. I pointed my laser at his head, planning his end at any hint of hostility. Instead, though, he pulled down his goggles and looked right into my viewing lens. I zoomed into his eyes, where I found not the terror I expected. It was almost a peace, or an acceptance, or even an expression of gentleness. After actions of such fire and passion, to be greeted like this confounded me, and I couldn't look away.

He started talking to the lens and I couldn't hear him, for the paladin was not equipped with audio broadcast capability. I had to know what he was saying though. My eyes glued to the camera, my control in hand, I cautiously approached the place of action. He caught sight of me and calmly said,

"I knew there must be someone at the helm of this one. The improvisation, the change in the gestures. It was far too impressive."

"Really?... Well, I've never seen anyone move like you either."

"Thanks. I mean I've looked at a few dismantled paladins, read about them, but never actually faced them until these last days."

"Yet somehow, you figured out how to stall them, without ever running one yourself? And did you make those tools you were using?"

"Yeah. I did. I've always loved making stuff. Figuring out how things work."

"So have I," I said unintentionally out loud.

"That makes sense. I see it in your fingers."

I looked down at my hands, slightly confused, and we both stayed quiet for a moment. When I looked up, I saw him still lying there, wounded and bloody, and felt a sharp regret for having done this to him. I then realized how caught up I'd been in the fight, and how much worse it could have gone. I met his eyes once more, but he just said, with warm smile,

"I'm Lancelot, by the way."

"I'm Galehaut," I responded quickly, as if by necessity.

"Nice to meet you, Galehaut. So, obviously you're in control of this army, and I'm in their way, so what do we do now?"

He was a sweaty, bleeding problem, lying in the dirt in front of me. One that no doubt would be easy to eliminate for anyone else in the Industrial Army. But I couldn't suppress that I saw in him the kid I once was and how I'd always longed to be. I impulsively took my controller, and shut off all the paladins. As the one in front of him, went dark and lowered its laser, he started to speak, but I cut him off, saying:

"You're hurt, so let me help. I have medical supplies up above in my ship. I promise, nothing will happen to you, and I'll bring you back tomorrow."

He looked at me inquisitively. Then finally, he nodded. "Okay, Galehaut. I believe you, but you're going to have to help me up because I'm pretty busted up and I'm not walking anywhere."

I lent him support, making our way to the landing pod, where we loaded up and headed back to the main ship. Re-attaching, we opened into the ship's inside. I couldn't help but notice his fascination with the whole interior of this minimal, no frills, cargo craft. He saw it as some grandiose technological masterpiece, asking me inquiries into the function of every knob and switch. His dazzled wonder was refreshing, but finally, I had to say:

"We'll have lots of time to talk about all of this, but first, let's clean you up, and then I'll patch up your surface wounds."

He nodded, still quietly eyeing his surroundings. I removed all my coverings and him out of his as well, then held him up while helping him shower off. The touch of this other human, in such a small space, was so unfamiliar, and so intimate. Someone who, until not long ago, was just a dot on my screen.

When we finished, I laid him out on the table and bandaged his harness wounds. I took out another tool, my modified creation, a fully functional x-ray, diagnostics and screen, with exceptional accuracy, and all in the palm of my hand. It didn't look pretty yet, wires sticking out and visible glue, but it served its function well. As I was reading Lancelot's body with it, he asked me:

"Did you make that thing?"

"I didn't make any of the programs, or invent the technology, but I modified it to this size and hooked it up to this screen. You see, my ship was a refurbished medical vehicle, and I saved all the tech when they ripped it out. Been playing with it ever since and creating lots of prototypes and devices just like this. Stuff that could maybe help other people out."

"That's impressive. I'd love to look at it when we're done. Don't worry. I won't steal your ideas."

"Oh, I don't care about that. I just want technology to exist and be available. If you can make it better, then go for it. We can both benefit."

"I like the way you think, Galehaut. Anyway, you wouldn't have to worry about me anyway. My experience with the digital side is very 21st century. But I'm learning whatever I can and I'm great with metal and wires!"

"That I can tell. Looking at the devices you've made, I'd say you're some kind of prodigy. Tell you what, let's share creations, right after I wrap your leg and shoulder up. Nothing's broken by the way. You'll just have to take it easy for a while."

With the medics done, so began an evening of exploration. First, through our technological creations. Sharing with each other's excited eyes and inquiring minds, how we created our devices from concept to execution, and even our ideas for future innovations.

Later in the night, we explored the rest of each other.

Where we'd come from. When we first discovered our passions. What we wanted to do in the future. How we cope with the difficulties surrounding us. Why, we were both so unfamiliar with such intimacy. And who we'd become; us two people whom yesterday should never have met, now falling asleep next to each other.

Waking up at sunrise, we shared breakfast, I gave him some of my clothes, and we fashioned him a crutch from random materials around us. Last night seemed like an impossible dream, but the connection still lingered and permeated the relative silence of morning.

It was me who finally broke it, in the pod back nearly back on the ground, asking one of the few questions that hadn't come up last night:

"I gotta know. What were you doing out there, anyway? All alone, fighting all these machines. You had to know that they would have killed you eventually?"

"I'll admit, Galehaut. I was alone because I was stubborn. There's a whole guild of us, warriors, and strategists, and innovators; all defenders of this land we call Camelot. All of us, including Arthur, our noble leader, wanted to defend our land, but Arthur calculated it out, and realized we couldn't defeat the paladins. They all made the choice to take the time they had, and prepare to leave our homes behind. I just couldn't do it though. I left our Round Table guild and went off on my own. I had to give my inventions a try. I couldn't cope with losing everything we had to the paladins once again."

"Once again? What do you mean? Paladins came through here before? What did they do?"

"You don't know? Well, yeah; every few years or even more often, they land in their pods, somewhere in Camelot, and mercilessly destroy everything in their path. Then the Industrial Army takes the resources they want, leaving most of the land scorched and unusable for years. So, you didn't even see what the machines you were controlling were doing?"

"I feel terrible saying this, but no. I never even thought about it. This was my first time on the ground. I spent my life looking at dots on a screen. Even when I was there yesterday, I was too distracted by you to really notice what was going on."

As we departed the pod, he said. "Let me show you something then."

I started to see the land around me. Broken fences. Barns and homes with burned out patches and laser holes shot in the walls. This scorched place could have so easily been where I grew up. Happily, I didn't see any bodies of any kind, but I couldn't help but worry about what lay beyond my sight. Certainly no one in the Industrial Army ever informed me of this kind of destruction. I then thought of all the numerous red dots I had watched become neutralized, and that hit me hard. I closed my eyes for a moment, not wanting to look around anymore. Suddenly though, Lancelot said:

"I knew the instant you walked over to me, that this wasn't about you, but I get it. It's a lot to be faced with all at once."

"I'm the controller! I dumped these machines here! Even if I was unaware of what they were really doing, I'm partially responsible for their destruction!"

"I know, Galehaut. But it's okay... May I just ask something of you real quick?"

"Uh. Sure. Anything."

"Open your eyes."

"What do you mean? My eyes are open."

"Good. So now you're aware, and that's the point. How you use that awareness from this point on is what really matters, not what happened in the past while you were in a state of unawareness. So what will you do now?"

"Well, I certainly won't endanger you or anyone else on this planet or elsewhere, so the Industrial Army's over for me. Beyond that, we'll have to dismantle all the paladins because even with this craft and the controls I have, the Industrial Army could come in here, override my power, and at any point, restart the destruction. At best, even if I fake my reports back to them and they don't catch on, they'll still wonder why this mission hasn't been completed in a couple of weeks. They'll inevitably come here, this time with a fugitive retrieval force. I just can't see much of an extended future for me, and I'm sad because after meeting you, I feel like a new life has just begun."

"Same. This is a new life for me too, and one that's worth protecting at all costs. I get that you're anxious about the future, but again, you just need to be able to see all the possibilities. You're not alone in this anymore. You know how the paladins work, and I have a device to stall them. Together, you and I, we'll make something bigger and more efficient, and if they come after us, we'll stop them in their tracks. Or maybe we can rewire them all! And not just you and I. There's the whole Round Table Guild to help us. We can use the paladins for our strength, and no longer will we have to be bullied out of our homes. We can truly stand up to them, and that's worth a try. What do you say, Galehaut?"

I can't help but smile at him. "Honestly, Lancelot, even if all I got out of this was just the one night with you, I still would have given up the rest of my life for it. I can't pretend that I'm not quaking inside, and I don't yet have within me the wherewithal to comprehend even the slightest hints at the unfolding of our future, but with you, any risk is worth it. My eyes are open now, and together, I see boundless potential. Whether we fail or not, this is the future we want, so let's go out there and make this a better universe!"

SCHEHERAZADE BIDS GOODNIGHT TO HER SISTER
by RJ Equality Ingram

They keep doves in the palace & release them
Ceremoniously each sunset to mark the work
Of women greeting husbands return from war
They light candles to hide the scent of sweat
In the red bedchambers while children watch
Maids turndown sheets warmed w/ stones
From the garden where their mothers weep
Silently mid prayer let us find all our answers
Among the hyacinth & roses whose oil we drop
Onto our pulse points our personal stigmata
Scheherazade bids goodnight to her sister
Then refuses the dagger they both smuggled
This far into her own unfinished fairytales
Standing together they ask for one last story

THE SEAFARER
by Geoffrey Heptonstall

An Evocation of Herman Melville

I seek to speak all I know
of my life at close quarters
in the ocean's experience,
having sailed its heartless swell,
its dark night of the deeps
even in the sight of land
and there the peaceable bounty.

My flesh is frost-withered
in cheerless chill deadening.
I feel my heart's hunger
that eats into the bone.
I am as one outcast,
a vessel ill-equipped for the crossing
ice-frozen in the worst of winter.

Homeless on the waves alone I hear
the roar that drowns the seabird's cry.
My compass needle is northward,
and this I follow as if favoured
by the fate of wished fortune,
an enterprise oceanwide.
The quest is for the sea's eternity.

The Marble Halls of Arts & Letters - book 1
by Timothy Arliss OBrien

"Odd how the creative power at once brings the whole universe to order."
Virginia Woolf

"The creative adult is the child who survived."
Ursula K. Le Guin

Preface
In the shadows of the marble walls,
where echoes of ancient whispers linger,

a dark arts college emerges,
a tapestry woven with ink and pigment.

Poets, composers, and painters alike,
gather in the sanctum of muses,

where the gods of old inspire
and the pursuit of knowledge
takes on a haunting form.

Chapter 1

I. Inception
In the realm of shadows,
where ink bleeds across parchment,
a college, shrouded in mystery,
emerges like a myth reborn.

Entrance gates are adorned with laurels
creating a portal to the arts unknown,
where poets weave words
into verses with the threads of forgotten tales.

In the orator's theater,
after the Muses convene, gather the poets,
with quills dipped in the essence of Hesiod's hymns,
compounding verses that echo through the ages,
an ode to contemplative wisdom,

In the darkened halls,
The Academy's genesis unfurls.

II. The Overture of Composers

Within the amphitheater of whispers
where notes become incantations,
composers gather in solemnity,
their minds alight with innovation and noise.
Apollo's lyre a spectral presence,
guides their symphony,
through the corridors of sound
where silence can become divinity.

Pergolesi, Massenet, Sibelius, Schnittke, and Glass
bring shades of ancient melodies,
and merge with modern discourse,
a fusion of motifs and harmonies.

In the classrooms, notes dance like ghosts in moonlight,
a cadence of unseen forces,
a sonic exploration into the deep dark midnights.

The pianist's fingers trace the constellations,
a celestial ballet in the dimmed studio of noise,
where composers reach to create stars,
their music the galaxies,
in the nocturnal embrace
to find every hidden auditory treasure.

III. The Canvas of the Painters

In the gallery of dreams, where hues breathe life,
painters wield brushes like sorcerers casting spells,
with palettes dipped in the pigments of mythic strife.
They summon titans and gods
upon canvases that glow and shimmer.

Goya, Bosh, and Breugel, as if spirits were invoked,
inspire and shine
in the haunting landscapes and ethereal strokes,
portraits of the Fates
and landscapes of the echoing Elysian Fields.
The Artists' true odyssey,
where the sacred and profane yield.
A Siren's Call, the masterpiece in shades of blue,
adorning the entrance to the studio of brushworks,
a canvas painted with the tears of a Muse.
The artists, conjurors of worlds unseen,
splash vivid hues everywhere they travel,
through the corridors of paint,
where we can see the surreal convene.

IV. The Poet's Society

Beneath the flickering lamps,
between the bookbinder's guild and the letterpress lab,
poets gather ink-stained and draped in shadows,
reciting verses that transcend earthly piety.

Their alchemy of words, those arcane echoes,
are akin to Sappho's whispers
and Dante's divine descent,

In the poet's courtyard,
an enclave where sonnets are set,
epic tales of love and loss, of gods and mortals,
are woven in stanvas, within these collegiate portals.
Milton, with his Paradise, that celestial maze,
guides them and leads them,
Through a darkened haze.

Deep within the Library, the poets scurry about,
with knowledge ablaze,
they commune with the ghosts of verse,
their words, a labyrinth,
where echoes converge into thoughtform.

V. The Darkened Atrium

In the heart of the college lies the botanist's atrium.
Panels of glass reaching for a darkening cold wet sky,
carrying the echoes
of philosophers and oracles entwined,
turning to the earth and her plants
for academics to meet Mother Gaia divine.
Statues of Demeter, Ceres, and Artemis,
stern in marble lurk amongst the greenery,
and guard the sacred space.
Fragrances of every magic grown here
waft through the marble halls.
The scent of inspiration,
plucked from the dirt can make its way below,
to the deep dark underground basement,
which houses the potion making workshop.
Then with an incantation of the poets of lore,
carried across campus from tower of spellcraft,
can turn a green leafy twig
into a gift from Hecate herself.
The Academy is under a spell, from education arcane,
where limited imagination is the only way to fail.

VI. The Ballad of Icarus
Within the halls, a tale unfolds,
a ballad of Icarus who at once arose.

A student ambitious, and hoping auspicious
reached for luminous, gratuitous, shimmer and shine.

Wings of waxen feather,
daring further and further in flight,
straight towards the sun of genius, a destiny in sight.

But hubris does whisper, such a seductive tune,
an ascent unchecked, now a faulty waxen cocoon.

Oh Icarus, ascending to ethereal height,
the waxen wings succumb to the solar light.
A fall from grace, the mortal Darwinian
Icarus descends, lost to oblivion.

A cautionary tale etched into the academy's lore,
the cost of avian genius,
that once past the ornithologist's aviary,
Icarus once soared.

VII. The Symposium of Shadows

Cassandra heard it first.
It sounded like the lecture on Socrates from last fall
(on the precursors of stoicism).
She heard it in the philosopher's study.
Unfortunately no one would believe her,
when she finally broke the silence and spoke up.

Only 1 person showed up for the meeting she called
Symposium of Shadows,
that spring in the astrologer's observatory.

The fates were sealed
because the oracles told the truth.

VIII. The Dionysian Revelry

Beneath the moonlit archways,
with tests complete, a Dionysian revelry,
with students dancing and singing, liberated and free.
Wine and verse flow a bacchanalian wave,
in the courtyard and hedge maze, an all night rave.

Full of abundance and lasting jubilations
The Academy let its spirit roam, full of congratulations.
A celebration of expression, and the magic of creativity,
what better way to celebrate
than an overdue weeklong festivity.

IX. The Oracle's Vision

Amidst the whispers and the nocturnal symphony,
an oracle emerges, veiled in prophecy.
She gazes into the cold dark mystic sea,
revealing the institution's fate, the vision: a decree.
"The Academy shall endure, a sanctuary of art,

where poets, composers, and painters depart,
but first they must yield a cosmic quest,
to keep their knowledge as a legacy,
in The Academy's chest."

X. The Twilight Sonata

As twilight descends upon darkened marble halls,
a sonata resonates through the ancient imaginative walls.
Composers, poets, and painters join a cosmic choir,
holding up their creations as immortal, in the realms of artistic fire.

The Academy must undergo a saga,
an epic tale in song and ink and paint,
to the tedious observation of the Muses,
so that gods and mortals may acquaint.

In this, the eternal pursuit of art,
the shadows shall wane,
and a symphony that is The Academy,
will be an ode
to the arts arcane.

Chapter 2

Act 1: The Gathering Storm
Scene 1: The Olympus Forum in Cyberspace
(Enter Zeus, Hera, Poseidon, Athena, Hephaestus, Ares, and Apollo in the virtual meeting room.)
Zeus: (Projecting thunderbolt holograms) Hear me, O gods of the digital realm! A storm is brewing in the mortal realm, and their affairs intertwine with our domain.
Hera: What troubles you, mighty Zeus?
Zeus: Mortals have entered the sacred space, wielding newfound powers.
They traverse their books of knowledge and command creation to be on their fingertips.
Poseidon: Mortals meddling with these ideas? This cannot be tolerated!
Athena: (Tapping into the creative airwaves) We must understand their intentions. Are they a threat or mere wanderers in the

wilderness?
Ares: I'd like to see them fight it out. I bet they are dying to know who among them is better than the rest.
Hephaestus: I have observed their creations - lyrics from the depths of the heart, melodies crafted better than I can forge, and visions from a brush I could not wield. They have entered our realm with their own forging.
Apollo: (Tuning his electric lyre) Let us watch and learn. Mortals, like us, have their own symphony. Perhaps they may bring an innovation to our pantheon.
Zeus: One might even rise as a demigod!

Scene 2: The Mortal Realm
at the Academy in the Library.
(Enter Phoebe, a scholar immersed in the dark arts, navigating the literary realm.)
Phoebe: (Inspecting her occult-inspired quill, tome, and scrying mirror) These may not be mere instruments, but are slowly becoming vessels of esoteric knowledge and fate. I must journey on and find what mysteries these conceal.
(Enter Perseus, a digital demigod, exploring the mortal world and The Academy.)
Perseus: Young scholar, the gods have been afraid before of the knowledge of mortals.
Phoebe: That is why we plan to paint ourselves as titans and lay claim to Olympus. We must climb!
(Perseus and Phoebe encounter a bookworm, a curse, slithering out from a nearby book.)
(Enter Medusa, a textual gorgon, muttering and whispering incantations)
Medusa: (Whispering in an eerie tone transfixed upon Phoebe) Scholar, you traverse realms beyond your grasp. Confront my gaze and meet your demise!
(Perseus lunges to Phoebe to knock her away from the stone-inducing gaze.)
(Phoebe drops her tome, quill, and scrying mirror and the mirror reflects Medusa's gaze back to her and shatters upon the floor.)
Phoebe: We must be more careful as of late, the oracles have spoken that strangeness is afoot and now we are down one scrying mirror.
(Phoebe invokes her mystical tome and quill, as her words are written, the retelling of the story transmutates into the precise words for magic to form. She realizes her enchanted quill has gained the power of spellcrafting.)

Phoebe: That bookworm curse was but a mere timeless peril cloaked in modern shadows. The ancient scholars must be informed of this.
Perseus: An ancient threat in a new form. The gods must know of this.

Act 2: The Pantheon's Debate
Scene 1: Olympus in the metaverse
(The gods convene again.)
Zeus: Mortals have entered the transcendent realm, seeking knowledge, power, and access to the deep arts. Perseus, the demigod among them, has encountered a threat, an ancient force reborn.
Hera: We must decide whether to aid or hinder these mortals in our domain.
Poseidon: They are like ants in the vastness of the artistic ocean. Shall we crush them or allow them to navigate the currents?
Athena: (Displays data analytics from the cloud) Mortals have potential. Their innovations could benefit both realms. We should guide them, not hinder.
Hephaestus: (Projecting digital blueprints) Mortals craft tools in our image. I see no harm in their forging, as long as they respect the balance.
Ares: I saw we don't hesitate any further. The power they wield is too strong and we must make them battle this out.
Apollo: (Strumming digital chords) Let us weave their fate into the cosmic music, but they must face the consequences of their actions.
Zeus: This is troubling sure, but they may be able to earn the magic.

Scene 2: The Mortal Realm
at the Academy's basement in the sanctum of recordings after a rehearsal.
(Perseus continues his journey, encountering a group of musicians.)
(Linus tunes his violin, Orpheus is running scales on his viola, and Thamyris struggles to get his cello back into its case.)
Linus: There is chaos also among the scribes.
Orpheus: Things haven't seemed calm with the artists in the gallery of dreams either. I had a watercolor class there yesterday and the colors were dull and weren't mixing like I remember from the last workshop with the Muses.
Thamyris: Whatever is happening is affecting the whole school.
(Perseus sends the conversation to Athena for her research.)
Perseus: Something is afoot and trouble seems to be brewing.
Athena: Perseus, demigod of the conquest, heed my counsel. Get out unseen and I will send my report to Hera and hopefully she can act

on your findings.

Act 3: The Rise of Chaos
Scene 1: Olympus on a conference call, yet again
(An ominous presence looms as Ares, the god of fighting online, manifests into a call with Hera and Zeus.)
Ares: Olympus is now made a playground for mortals, and I shall turn their haven into chaos!
Hera: Ares, cease your actions! The mortal realm is not your battleground.
Ares: Mortals and gods alike will bow before the might of my chaos and confusion. I am the architect of this chaos and the mortals will fall, lest it happen to Olympus.
How dare they come for our power!

Scene 2: The Mortal Realm
hidden amongst the plants in the botanist's atrium.
(Perseus witnesses the havoc wreaked by Ares.)
Perseus: (Screaming at the gods) Ares has unleashed chaos upon the mortal realm. We must unite to stop him!
Athena: (Guiding Perseus) Seek Hephaestus in the forge. He may need help creating a weapon to counter the chaos.
(Perseus ventures to the forge in virtual reality.)
Hephaestus: The chaos comes from rivalry and the need to one-up and gain a win against one another. It's wrecking the creative underbelly of the mortal realm and threatens to stamp out imagination from the mortal fabric. It's a gift that was stolen by Prometheus that is now interwoven through all of human history.
Perseus: Any idea of what may defeat this chaos and return the balance?
Hephaestus: I've almost finished forging a sword with a thousand sparks of creativity and stones from the Library of Alexandria. It may cut through the chaos if you can wield it well.
Perseus: I will try my best. Hera transferred the spreadsheets and infographics on the chaos to Athena.
(Hephaestus sends the sword of divine knowledge and sparking-inspiration to Olympus and Perseus.)
Hephaestus: You were once a mere mortal, but now a demigod with all of our hope. This sword holds the power to cleanse the chaotic corruption wrought by Ares.

Act 4: The Final Clash
Scene 1: Olympus online

(The gods prepare for the final confrontation with Ares.)
Zeus: (Summoning digital lighting) Ares, your chaos will not prevail. Olympus will endure, and a bridge will be built so mortals shall learn as much as they can.
Ares: (Surrounded by clouds of chaos) The age of unity between gods and mortals will end. It has been foretold by the oracles, Zeus. Mortals will fail, and the mortal realm shall be reshaped by aggression with wars over the very ideas they are learning now. They will never have what we have.

Scene 2: The Mortal Realm at the Academy in the hedge maze.
(Perseus confronts Ares as they are both lost in the maze.)
Perseus: (Wielding the sword from the gods) Ares, your chaos ends here. The mortals will continue to climb Olympus and will build their destiny with newfound wisdom and creativity.
(A battle ensues and the mortal realm trembles with the clash against the surrounding chaos.)
Perseus: (Raising the sword to make the final strike) It's time for this chaos to end.
(Perseus uses the sword to cut through the clouds of confusion. Ares shrinks back, and accidentally stumbles into the trapdoor.)
Ares: (Falling through the hedge trap maze into the underground.) This isn't over! I will escape this trap and make the mortals pay!
Perseus: Chaos may be eternal, but the mortal realm will know peace and those imaginative creatives may struggle for generations to climb Olymbpus, but they will come to know what they have. It's special, it's accessible, it's magic.
(The gods shine down on Perseus in celebration.)

Act 5: The New Era
Scene 1: Olympus in person this time.
at a big table, covered in a feast, surrounded by clouds.
(The gods reflect on the events.)
Zeus: Mortals have proven themselves capable of navigating the creative expanse. Our realm shall evolve with their innovations. May they grow ever closer in union with us.
Hera: We must hope the mortals use caution. Should their wit fail to precede their imagination their creativity may falter.
Athena: (Observing data trends) Mortals learn and adapt quickly. With guidance, they may bring balance to our two realms.
Hephaestus: May we learn from the tools and mediums they create and use to evolve their own consciousness.
Apollo: (Strumming a hopeful melody) The cosmic harmonies weave

a tale of collaboration between gods and mortals, of innovation and wisdom shared.

Scene 2: The Mortal Realm
at the Academy in the poet's courtyard.
(Perseus stands victorious with the sword of divine knowledge and sparking inspiration, surrounded by creative scholars and professors.)
Perseus: Let this be a lesson for both mortals and gods. In the vastness of imagination, harmony can prevail if we forge our destinies with wisdom and collaboration.

(The mortal realm transforms, integrating the lessons learned, growing more powerful with mortals and gods coexisting in the ever-evolving landscape of the imagination age.)

(As the curtain falls, sparks of imagination flicker and fall illuminating the stage, symbolizing the balance of gods and mortals. The gods feast at a table on one side of the stage and the students from the Academy adhere to their studies on the other side of the stage.)

The cosmic balance has been restored.

Chapter 3: An epilogue on the ongoing cosmic balance.

At the edge of the fruitful lands,
    raging against the sea,
        shrouded in perpetual mist,

  there stood an institution unlike any other—The Academy.

Towering spires,
    cloaked in ivy and mystery,
        reached towards the heavens
            as if trying to pierce the veil
                between the mortal and the divine.

This dark academic bastion,
    a crucible for creativity,
        where arts are cultivated,
            builds to a fervor bordering on the arcane.
The Academy's origins

        are veiled in myth and whispers,
                like the fog that clung to its periphery.

Some claimed it had risen
        from the ashes of the ancient world,
    an echo of the bygone eras
        when gods walked among mortals.
            Others believed it was a clandestine society,
              (born from the shadows)
                    harnessing the raw power of inspiration
                lingering in the air.

The students who sought entry,
        a diverse assembly,
            were drawn from the far reaches of the artistic spectrum.
    Painters with eyes that reflected
the hues of the underworld,
        Poets who spoke in riddles that echoed through time,
    Composers who plucked chords that resonated
with the whispers of forgotten deities
        They all found sanctuary
            within the hallowed halls of The Academy.

The curriculum became an intricate tapestry
        woven with threads of mythology,
            infusing the institution in mystery.
The students delved into the timeless tales of gods and heroes,
        seeking inspiration from the divine dramas that unfold in the
                                  celestial realms.
The study of ancient myths was not a mere academic exercise
        but a communion with the very essence of creativity,

a rite that bound
        the aspirants
            to the mystical forces
                that coursed through The Academy's
foundations.
At the heart of the institution,
        underground in the sanctum of the muses
            (adorned with frescoes depicting forgotten epics),
                students gathered to pay homage to the Muses.

Nine ethereal figures,

embodiments of inspiration,
    guided the artistic pursuits of those
      who dared to tread
    the labyrinthine corridors of The Academy.

Yet, amidst the divine guidance,
    a shadowy figure lurked
    (a teacher with an enigmatic presence)
    and sent shivers down the spines of even the boldest students.
Professor Moros,
    named after the god of impending doom,
      a master of the esoteric arts.
His classes delved into the darker corners of creativity,
    exploring the fine line between brilliance and madness.

Under the watchful gaze of Professor Moros,
    students studied the tragic fates

of those touched by artistic genius.

The stories of Icarus,
    who soared too close to the sun on wings of wax,
and cursed Cassandra,
    plagued with foresight but fated never to be believed.
Each one served as a cautionary tale.

Moros believed that true artistic brilliance
    required a willingness to confront the abyss,
     to dance on the edge of sanity,
    and to grapple with the shadows that lurked within the soul.
The Academy's library,
    a dark haunted repository
      of ancient tomes and forbidden knowledge,
    held secrets that even the most daring students hesitated to
                    unveil.

It was rumored that the library's guardian,
    a spectral figure known as Mnemosyne,
       guarded not only the knowledge contained within
         but also the very fabric of memory and inspiration.

Those who sought to delve too deep
    risked losing themselves in the endless corridors of forgotten dreams.
Legends spoke of a hidden chamber
    (within the labyrinthine depths of the academy).

A chamber where the very essence of inspiration
was said to be distilled into an elixir
that granted unparalleled creative prowess.

The Elixir of Euterpe, named after the Muse of tragedy,
was both coveted and feared.
Those who imbibed its intoxicating essence
were rumored to become vessels
for forces beyond mortal comprehension.
In the dim glow of flickering torches,
    students gathered in secret societies,
        reciting incantations and exchanging forbidden knowledge.

They sought to unlock the mysteries of The Academy,
    to transcend the boundaries between the mortal and the divine,
    and to wield the power of inspiration like a double-edged sword.
As whispers of The Academy spread beyond the valley,
    artists and seekers from distant lands sought the elusive institution.

They braved treacherous paths, navigated uncharted waters,
    and faced trials that tested the very fabric of their beings.

For those deemed worthy,
    the gates of the academy opened,
        revealing a world where the line
    between reality and myth
blurred into a dreamscape of endless possibilities.

And so,
    The Academy stood as a beacon in the artistic cosmos,
        a crucible where mortals dared to dance with gods,
        where the echoes of ancient myths
        resonated in every brushstroke, stanza, and note.

In the eternal twilight of its existence,
    The Academy continued to beckon
        to those who hungered for the sublime,
            the forbidden, and the divine.

These are the correspondences of what we've seen within the marble halls.

More books on the marble halls are to be written
        with many more stories to be told.

Van Gogh's Night
by Lynette Esposito

Before he loved the stars
He loved the paint, the brush, the canvas
He loved the ear he sacrificed
He probably loved a woman
We cannot go back in time
and see what drove him
But if love is a key to everything,
Why did he love the night?

To William Wordsworth
by James B. Nicola

"The child fathers the man?"
                            'Tis true!
But note: the child is never through—

whence springs so much of tragedy
and comedy
        like you
                and me.

At the State Fair
by Marianne Taylor

Most of the fairgoers observed the comely woman
robed like a statue in layers of gossamer cloth
fair hair plaited and piled. She strode down the midway

past lights that flashed and jangled, music tangled
and tuneless. She paused to stare at the Ferris wheel
arcing like a rainbow, tracked the buckets

bobbing against dark sky. Then felt a tug
near her knee, looked down to see a toddler
reaching up, fists sticky with webs of pink.

She picked her up and moved along, long
strides steady on dusty earth. Surely a few
noticed the sheaves and stalks embroidered in silk

on her gown, guessed her a part of the pageantry
no doubt. In the Ag Exhibit Hall she bowed
before the enormous Butter Cow until

the restless child complained. Pictures of corn
wheat, and beans, but no plants? Powders and sprays
chemists in coats. What would Triptolemus say?

Offered gifts of soda, deep-fried Snickers
they ate, baby wiping gooey fingers
 in her hair. Amidst the livestock she took her ease

released the child who shrieked at thousand pound
pigs, angora bunnies, their tricky pink eyes.
After blasts of fireworks styled a la Zeus

in the stable housing Clydesdales, behind piles
of hay they slept. And early in the morning
Demeter rose and kissed the child, then left.

Henna
by John Delaney

The process of this tattoo-making
requires a steady hand, unshaking,
so a continuous line can be laid
down by the needle's glass blade.

Precisely like a surgeon's scalpel,
but above the skin,
this moving line will begin
almost feeling palpable

of the practitioner's art:
she, who draws from imagination
and an experienced heart
a unique creation.

The brown dye stain that remains gradually fades
away in shades like a beautiful memory.

In Morocco, henna tattoos are most common on the hands and feet. They are thought to bring good luck.

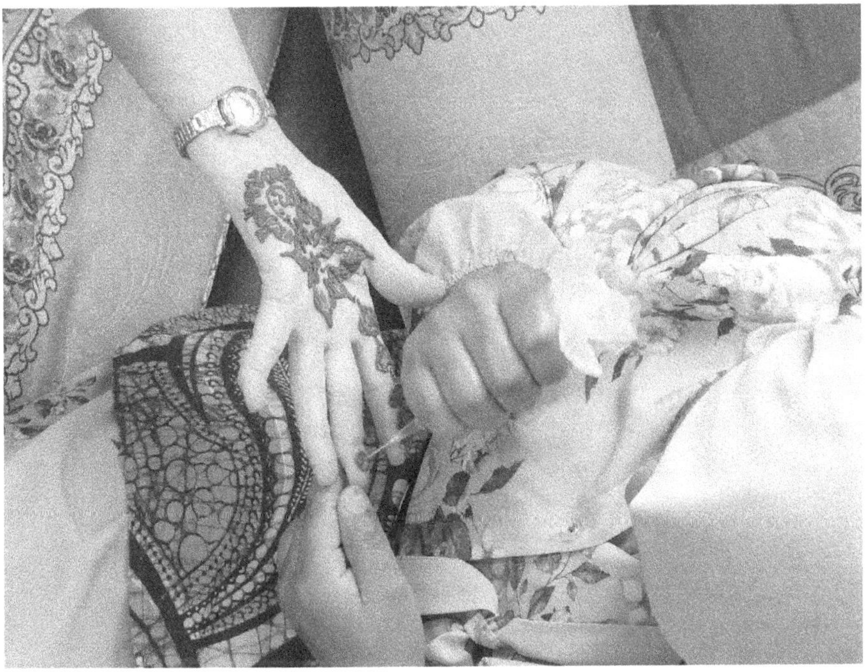

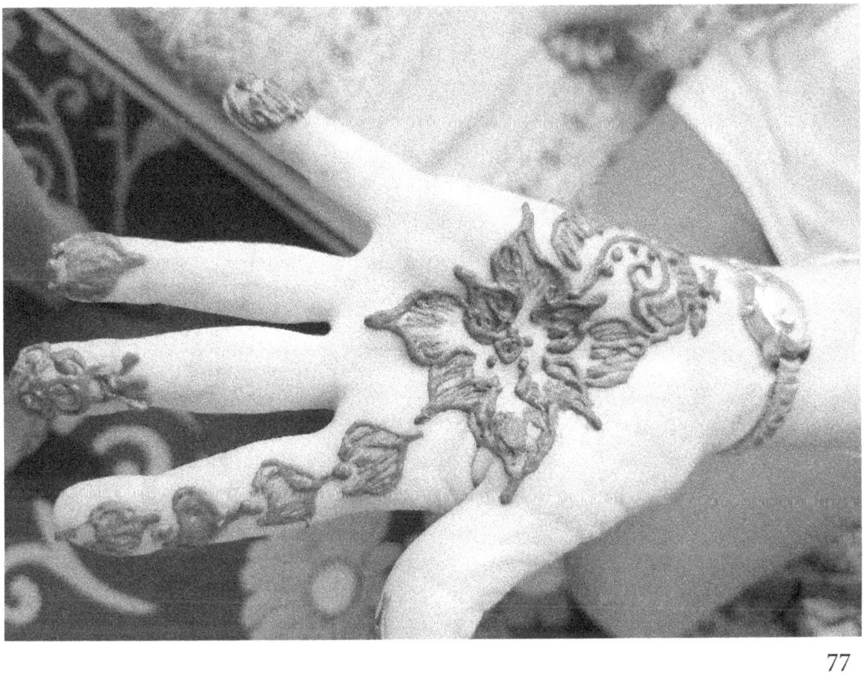

First of the Slut-Shamed: A Hymn for Helen of Troy
by Ivy Jong

Hello, Helen.

  Helen Harlot, Helen Home-Wrecker, Helen Whore. Most beautiful woman in the world, hatched from a swan's egg, product of yet another rape perpetrated by your divine slut of a father, the "omnipotent" thunderer. His many bedfellows tell a different story.

  In all the myths, you are glittering, resplendent. And always, always, you are being taken.

  Women all around you are constantly being turned into plants and beasts, chased, abducted, vaporized to ash, raped and then killed in a jealous rage. But none so much as you. Men cannot seem to keep their hands off you. When you are a child, less than ten years old, the great "hero" Theseus kidnaps you for marriage. Your brothers have to fight their way through a city to bring you home. Not a decade of life and already a victim of pedophilia, child-trafficking, sexual slavery. Why have I known your name since childhood yet not learned of this story until now, years later? History does not want you known as Helen the Child Bride, you are Helen the Slut. It is fine for your father, but not you. For a man in your world, sex is a domination, an assertion of power. For a woman, it is a transgression. A sin.

  When you finally come of marriageable age, men come crawling out of every hidden crack and dusty corner of Greece to bargain over the right to possess you, like a prized cow. The one who wins you isn't even present; he sends his brother to haggle for you in his absence and wins because his coffers are filled with the most gold. Your father hands over your leash without hesitation, counting the coins with wide eyes. This newest husband is rough and his beard scratches, but you cannot complain. You are his property now. You are a teenager.

Even the possession laws of men do not save you from another abduction. This time some prince rapes you and drags you across the ocean, starting a war in the process. Hordes of men flock to Troy to fight over you, to reclaim your husband's "property" and their pride, so very fragile. Ten years and hundreds of dead men later, the war is over, the prince is in his grave, and you are handed back to the Spartan king—returned to your rightful owner. Always being bought or stolen, changing hands, carted from place to place. Whenever you look behind you, your footprints stain the ground with your former owner's blood. But you are not the knife, nor the hand that wields it. You are the pilfered cattle, the object of argument that incites the murder. The blood is not on your hands, it only stains you from proximity. People do not blame cattle. But you are a woman, and that is enough.

In every retelling of your tale there are women pointing their fingers at you to save themselves. So many tell your story for you, but no one ever asks your opinion. No one permits you a voice. Now I ask you,

When you pushed through the white membrane and shattered the eggshell, new hands grasping for air, did you know you would be blamed for ten years of bloody war, the destruction of a great city, the deaths of hundreds of men, for your own abduction and rape? If you had known, would you have crawled back inside and sealed the fragments of egg closed again with your own spit and blood, with the birth fluids still clinging to your newborn skin?

Did you know that other women would point to you as the most vile of your sex? That not even they, those Grecian girls who had been nothing but things to be raped by gods and stolen by men, would raise a voice in defense of you, but instead against you? Harlot, homewrecker, bitch, slut, whore. Barbed words aimed at you like arrows, your abductions and rapes held against you like knives. Every direction you turned, sharp and unforgiving. Everything that happened to you was because you flaunted your beauty, because you tempted them. You wanted it. You asked for this.

Did you ever think of slashing your face, of scarring it beyond recognition? Of jumping from a bridge and diving deep into the stone-hard waters, down further and further until you washed up on the black shores of Hades? Or would that have been self-mutilation, and grounds for banishment to the pits of eternal screams? These gods, always so clever with their sins. They don't like to let their playthings slip away so easily. But perhaps your revenge lies in that you lived. Every time they say your name—no matter what unsavory titles follow—at least they will never forget how many you dragged down with you.

town crier
by Aletha Irby

*Stay close to any sounds that
make you glad to be alive.* Hafiz

through the morning
still silenced by darkness
your sudden eruption
allegro
arpeggio
appoggiatura
joyful enough
to resurrect icarus
to enjoin him nidicolous
to soar forth once again
airborne on wingéd rhapsody
oh songbird
you remind us
that we can never fly
too close to the sun
and i too rise
fledged by your warbling
which welcomes me
with ebullient
unambivalent simile
as if i were the dawn

for Isabel Davis Neese

Bluebeard's Greatest Lie: A Creative Latin Composition Inspired by Carmen Maria Machado's In the Dream

by Heather Hambley

Mendacium[1] Blavabarbae maximum erat quod fuit una atque unica regula[2]: uxorem novissimam aliquid quod cuperet[3], dummodo illud solum libidinosumque — non figere[4] pusillam clavem in pusillam seram — ne ea ageret[5], agere posse.

At vero hoc fuisse modo principium, modo probationem scimus. Uxor cecidit (atque ut fabulam narraret[6] haec similis mei[7] vixit), sed etiamsi[8] approbata esset, fuisset alia petitio, paulo[9] maior vel paulo inusitatior, ac si se fingi[10] — velut[11] fanatica cingulorum mediam partem corporis minus minusque vellicat — sivisset, spectaculum fuisset in quo Blavabarba cum uxorum praeteritarum putrescentibus cadaveribus in manibus suis saltabat[12] atque uxor novissima crescentem horrorem comprimens sorbensque ovum vomitus in pectore trementis mute sedebat.

Cum[13] haec ab clave condicionibusque non refugisset, nec istum dicentem[14] gradus uxoris esse graviores interpellavisset, nec stupranti[15] lacrimantem contra dixisset, nec recusavisset ei suadentem ut taceret[16], nec contundentem bracchia locuta esset, nec tractantem eam parem cani infantive obiurgavisset, nec postremo ululans petensque auxilium in pagum proximum per semitam ex castello cucurrisset — ita rationale videbatur illam ibi sessuram esse ac virum cadaver quartae uxoris versantem spectaturam esse[17], cuius caput putre in carnis cardine[18] retro recumbebat.

Uxor novissima secum reputat: per omnia te confirmari et tenacitatem amoris exerceri[19].
Filia dulcis, probaris approbarisque. Vide[20] quam bona fidelisque sis atque quantopere ameris[21].

[1] Dear Muses, be with me — I really hope I pulled this off! I wanted to reflect the restrictions and complexities of Bluebeard's conditions throughout this composition structurally, so I often opt for hypotaxis over parataxis, using a lot of participial phrases and subordinate clauses. I'll try to signal the syntactically sticky spots here.
[2] *quod fuit...regula:* a substantive clause consisting of *quod* and the indicative can translate as 'that' or 'the fact that'; introduces an indirect statement *uxorem...agere posse*
[3] *quod (ea) cuperet:* relative clause of characteristic, antecedent is *aliquid*
[4] *non figere...seram:* infinitive phrase in apposition with *illud*
[5] *dummodo...ne ea ageret:* a negative proviso clause subordinated within the indirect statement, whee!
[6] *ut...narraret:* a natural result clause
[7] Thank god you did, Carmen Maria Machado. *In the Dream House* tells the story of her experience in an abusive partnership. This comp is inspired by my favorite chapter: "*Dream House as Bluebeard.*" *Mei* is the only direct mention of Machado in this chapter, although of course I believe her closing address *Filia dulcis,* 'Sweet girl' includes herself (and me and anyone else who has ever believed the lie that love needs to be earned, endured).
[8] Hark, two past contrary-to-fact conditionals! (1) [pro] *etiamsi approbata esset,* [apo] *fuisset alia petitio, ac* (2) [pro] *si sivisset,* [apo] *spectaculum fuisset.* Translates 'had...'would have'
[9] ablative of degree of difference with the comparative adjectives
[10] *fingi,* a present passive infinitive depending on *sivisset,* can mean to be mentally formed by instruction (ie, 'to be trained' or 'taught') or to be shaped in the physical sense, like a work of art or a statue (ie, 'to be fashioned' or 'modeled'). Both meanings are at play, as Bluebeard is molding his newest wife both physically and psychologically.
[11] Machado compares the newest wife's training to that of a corset fanatic — I think about this simile all the time
[12] switching to the indicative here to turn up the vividness of this vomitous scene
[13] *Cum haec non refugisset, nec interpellavisset, nec contra dixisset, nec recusavisset, nec locuta esset, nec obiurgavisset, nec cucurrisset* are all translated causally.
[14] *dicentem,* a present active participle modifying *istum,* introduces the indirect statement *gradus eius esse graviores*; the comparative predicate adjective *graviores* can be translated 'too heavy'
[15] Continue to supply substantive forms of *iste* (Bluebeard), smothered in contempt, with each upsetting present active participle *stupranti, suadentem, contundentem, tractantem.*
[16] *ut taceret:* indirect command dependent on *(istum) suadentem*
[17] *sessuram esse* and *spectaturam esse* are both future active infinitives depending on *videbatur rationale,* 'it seemed logical that she would...'
[18] *in carnis cardine,* 'on a hinge of flesh' — so gruesome! Fun distinction I learned: *caro* strictly translates to 'meat,' whereas *viscus* denotes 'living flesh.' So definitely gotta use *caro* here.
[19] Technically this should probably be direct speech, but I chose an indirect statement because I wanted her reasoning to feel more rehearsed, conditioned per fn. 10.
[20] *Vide,* 'Look' introduces two indirect questions.
[21] May I suggest closing this reading with a listen to Kendrick Lamar's *Crown.* Sweet girl, *love gon' get you killed.*

Glossary

ago, -ere, egi, actus, *to do*
approbor, -ari, -atus, *to pass the test*
Blavabarba, -ae, m. *Bluebeard*
cadaver, -eris, n. *corpse*
cado, -ere, cecidi, casus, *to fail*
canis, -is, mf. *dog*
cardo, -inis, m. *hinge*
cingulum, -i, n. *corset, girdle, chastity belt*
clavis, -is, f. *key*
comprimo, -ere, -pressi, -pressus, *to suppress*
confirmo (1), *to strengthen*
contra dicere, *to protest against* (c. dat)
contundo, -ere, -tudi, -tusus, *to bruise*
cresco, -ere, crevi, cretus, *to grow, increase*
curro, -ere, cucurri, cursus, *to run, fly, hasten*
etiamsi, conj. *even if*
exerceo, -ēre, -ui, -itus, *to train, cultivate, practice*
fidelis, -e, *loyal, faithful*
figo, -ere, fixi, fixus, *to fix, stick*
gradus, -us, m. *step*
interpello (1), *to interrupt*
inusitatus, -a, -um, *strange, uncommon, unusual*
lacrimo (1), *to weep, cry*
libidinosus, -a, -um, *arbitrary*
loquor, loqui, locutus sum, *to mention, speak of*
media pars corporis, *waist*
mendacium, -i, n. *lie*
minus, adv. *smaller*
modo, adv. *just, only, merely*
obiurgo (1), *to scold, rebuke*
pagus, -i, m. *village*
par, paris, equal, *like* (c. dat)
pectus, pectoris, n. *breast*
peto, -ere, -ivi, -itus, *to plead (for)*
praeteritus, -am -um, *past, prior*
probo (1), *to test*
pusillus, -a, -um, *tiny, insignificant*
puter, -tris, -tre, *decaying, rotting*
quantopere, adv. *how much, with how great effort*
recumbo, -ere, -cubui, *to loll*
recuso (1), *to decline, refuse*
reputo (1), *to reflect upon, reason*
salto (1), *to dance*
sedeo, -ēre, sedi, sessus, *to sit*
semita, -ae, f. *path*
sera, -ae, f. *lock*
sino, -ere, sivi, situs, *to allow, let*
sorbeo, -ēre, -ui, *to swallow, bear*
stupro (1), *to defile, rape*
suadeo, -ēre, -si, -sus, *to urge, persuade* (c. dat)
taceo, -ēre, -cui, -citus, *to be silent, shut up*
tracto (1), *to treat*
ululo (1), *to wail, scream, shriek*
uxor, uxoris, f. *wife*
-ve, conj. (enclitic) *or*
vellico (1), *to pinch*
velut, adv. *just as*
verso (1), *to spin, whirl about*

SCHEHERAZADE BIDS GOODNIGHT TO HER SONS
by RJ Equality Ingram

Remember that words have power when spun
The way they turn spider silk into tapestries
Remember your enemies laugh themselves
Onto the floor for the same reasons as you
Remember the sound of my voice as I rocked
Each of you to sleep during the rainstorms
If I cannot see you off to be married do love
The way your father & I loved you & promise
Her nothing we would never promise to you
Remind your children that it never gets darker
Than the night as a broken heart heals itself
Remember there is a piece of sand for each
Moment I have loved telling you my stories
Now rest up for tomorrow's fresh adventure

To Have and To Hold
by Miles Kenny

I.

On a hill in the northwest corner of the ancient Athenian Agora, the Temple of Hephaestus is pocked with bullet holes. The little craters of exact proportion stand in stark contrast to the more natural degradations of time on the Dorian columns, those marks of erosion on marble like the jagged teeth of some primordial being. The pockmarks signal a rational destruction, a testament to humanity's ability to destroy itself faster and with more accuracy than any god or demon. They are a fitting tribute to Hephaestus, the cripple god of craft, irrespective of their providence. The bullet holes could be said to be the culmination of a several hundred-year process, an effort to mold a Southern Balkan nation long attached to the Ottoman Empire into Europe's Eden, the foreign homeland which had for so long eluded the new masters of the world. But, in another sense, their origin was quite straightforward. The bullet holes in Hephaestus's temple originated from machine guns fired from the hill underlying the Acropolis, from where British forces sought to extricate the Greek Partisans taking cover in the temple.

The partisans, who had fought alongside the British against the Italian Fascists and the German Nazis in years past, had learned the lessons of combat in the ancient city. They had learned that the hovels and tenements where most of them lived could be torn to shreds with modern automatic weapons, but the marble buildings of the ancients? They were resilient. No one worried much about the building's significance; there were more pressing concerns. Athenians had always lived among the ruins of the past, they were used to conversions of structures from temples to churches to mosques and back again as meaning was imposed upon them.

It was the British and the Germans, though these ones (usually) without machine guns, that seemed hellbent on turning the city into a museum, and the process was relatively new. It had been less than 15 years since the American School of Classical Studies in Athens had bought the strip of land in the central city and declared it the Agora, a sacred space to be left untouched by time, and evicted and demolished entire neighborhoods which sat on top of their discovery. Some of the partisans under Hephaestus's protection had probably lived in now-vanished buildings at the foot of the hill, after and before the Agora was the Agora. Between taking cover and returning fire, the partisans probably didn't consider the irony that it wasn't the horrors of occupation and civil war that had disappeared their homes, but rather a peculiar thing called "historical preservation."

The temple receives fewer visitors than some of the nearby attractions. Take, for instance, a mossy foundation sitting just beyond the formal bounds of the Agora, which, since 1976, has been called the Prison of Socrates. Socrates's prison was in fact first excavated in 1949, as the last of the partisans from up on the hill were rounded up and sent to island prisons, but it was not until the democratic era that an American archeologist, after rereading Plato's Crito, noticed two conspicuous features in the otherwise anonymous structure. He noticed a room with a bath, which Socrates is said in the dialogue to have used, and he noticed thirteen small jars, the exact kind, he reasoned, which would have been necessary for the systematic administration of the hemlock poison that the philosopher used to end his life. Thus, Socrates' prison was born. To look at Socrates's prison and experience it as such is to look at a line of stones and imagine the building that grew from it, imagine the people who came and went, and the person who never left. It is to imagine the philosopher as a mortal of flesh and blood whose temporal life was and then was not. It is a powerful exercise in radical empathy and in the decentering of the sensual perception of a thing's existence towards an ephemeral reality in which ghosts are real and omnipresent. It is an exercise which, if done correctly, makes the line of stones entirely superfluous.

II.

Today's Athens is a city of museums, and you can trace the history of Greece, the middle east, and the entire world if you spend long enough in their halls. But there are limitations. To the English speaker in Athens, history ends in the year 1944. The Athens War Museum traces the greatness of Hellenistic martial prowess from the Spartans and Macadoneans all the way through to the heroics of the Greek soldiers of the Second World War. Of course, the Greek military is humble about their great victories of the second half of the 20th century: the wars against farmers and laborers, the war against democracy. The museum, in its personal history, is a testament to papered over divides and negotiated amnesias. The museum's establishment was decided by the Greek parliament in 1967, when that body served under the watchful eye of the colonels and their allied royal family, and the museum was finally inaugurated in 1975, after both had been expelled, its opening presided over by Konstantinos Tsatsos, the first elected president of Greece to serve a full term. It was as if to give the military their museum was to imprison them in it, to replace the body which had served as an authoritarian modernizing force, the Latin junta, with an apolitically patriotic one, the European military.

November 17th is commemorated as the end of the military dictatorship and the return of democracy in Greece. It marks the last day of the Polytechnic Uprising, when students at Athens premier university protested for the return of democracy and were gunned down by tanks in the courtyards of academic buildings. There are monuments and plaques remembering the uprising, but its most important commemoration was written in law, a statute banning police and military from college campuses in all but the most dire of circumstances. In 2019, after a decade of civil unrest and legitimacy-bleeding left wing governments, the newly-elected right wing New Democracy party repealed the law.

Despite the nominally legitimate nationalist bent to the November 17th commemoration, it is more or less the exclusive purview of the left. In Athens it is marked by a march in which I saw more red flags in one place than in any other moment of my life. At the head of the march are the survivors of the original uprising, followed in turn by the labor unionists and respectable leftists, with the anarchists and the general milieu of black-bloc/crust-punk types making up the rear. The march ends at the American Embassy, and after a while the elderly and respectable types disperse, leaving only the anarchists and armored police to stage their ritual combat, a pastiche of pitched battle that lets both groups quench their thirst for the real thing. A tattoo artist I knew described the night as "a load of fun… After they pushed us to Exarchia, they left us alone… by the end of the night everyone was drunk and sleeping with each other."

III.

Writing on ancient buildings comes in many forms. Inscriptions, written in a bizarre first person, announce "I am a boundary rock. I serve to demarcate the limits of the city of Athens and I was laid in the time of Pericles." Others form fragments, in the Christian dark ages the means and skill to mine marble were lost, and old buildings were stripped of stone for the building of the new. It is for this reason that a Byzantine church might announce on its exterior walls a broken and half-erased dedication to Phoebus Apollo. But it was a third style of marking I found the most transfixing. Crude script on marble walls with cruder meanings, graffiti of times past, the bored scribbles of children and soldiers announcing themselves to history, marking their friendships and loves, but, more often than not, reveling in simple obscenity, penning broken verses on throbbing cocks, marking a wall without the intention of leaving a legacy for future generations, but because the wall was close by.

I remember Athens in these ways and others. I remember Athens in the smell of the Old Spice I was using when I was there, in flashes out a car window, in music in the streets, and in the worst weed I've ever smoked. I remember conversations in cafes where cigarette smoke wafted and English was used because it was the common language among the Afghans and the

Serbs. I remember crushing feelings of loneliness. I remember uneven sidewalks and dog shit everywhere and broken drain systems which would dump gray water down onto the sidewalk. I remember the brief period before sunrise when the city truly ground to a halt, when the streets held a sublime stillness and the apartment buildings could have been empty for a thousand years.

Near the end of my time in Greece I took a short trip to the island of Lesbos. I went for a morning swim where the edge of Asia was visible on the horizon and found in the sea a red rectangle, seemingly of terracotta, which had a deep groove running longways through its center. I realized it was shindling, probably not from Sappho's house, but conceivably Roman in origin, quite ancient to be sure. I dried it off and packed it away. I was going to give it to someone I loved. Something special, a thing to have and to hold, direct evidence of a communion with time and space, a talisman connecting then and now and there and here and her and I. But when I was leaving the hotel to board that propeller plane through a Mediterranean storm I paused, and I dropped the thing in the grass. When I got back to Athens I stopped in at a tourist trap in Plaka and bought her a t-shirt that had emblazoned on the chest, "I don't need Google, my mother-in-law knows everything." It was stupid, sure, but I remember how she laughed when she read it.

Girls in Winter Triptych
by Kate Falvey

I. Alice Everlasting

Sure, the Dodo had its race
and I got my thimble back
but pattern recognition
has been daunting ever since,
the air marked by so much passing,
blurry with regret. It's hard to trust
a shape, a beginning or an end,
when all is crossing borders trailing ghosts
of other minds and the remnants of pretend.
I'm not sure who I am or how I begin or end
or how I lasted for so long in worlds so
not my own. I've always been alone, always
tipped toward tracing paradox as I ran
with scissors blunted -- sharpened? --
by my need to trim the wind out of my tales.

II. Wendy's Good to Go

I didn't mean to grow
so far from the lagoon
and the little patch
of underground distortion
where the cakes and tales
are ever weeping
in the dank and dirty dark.

There wasn't more than fly-by-night
assurance of safe harbor
but the dream of it was certainly
a lark, the cutlass and the drumbeat
and those murky mermaids calling to the moon
were over all too soon,
though I panicked at the time.

Sneaking night flights from the rift
of nursery and watchdog was sublime
though that fairy freaked the stars
with a luminous ill will.
If gossamer could kill, I'd be there still,
a crushed voice hovering blurrily
in a current of pretend.

But I kept savagery at bay
with prissy allegiance to all the rules I knew
and most of them could bend.

III. Nancy's Last Caper

Ned's scrawny yoga-posing wife, younger than him
by twenty or so years, is onto richer pickings and so
locked him in a home, claiming he's a hazard to himself,
lying that he's left the burners on and mistook her for a cat
burglar or the rat she really is. The home is not so homey, no
surprise, though she pitched it to him with a pout and shifty
teary eyes. Ned always was a prize pushover and now he falls
for outright lies, his penchant for clumsy gallantry abetting
his demise. So I swoop down to the Sea Breeze in Cape Coral
disguised as his attorney in a snit and razzle the conniving little twit,
spring Ned from the trap of his own beleaguered brain, and
embolden him to take the reins and light out for a final spin
before both of us succumb to haunting clocks and inns.

MEASURE RESTORED
by Geoffrey Heptonstall

An Evocation of Elizabethan Drama

We look in the world's eye
to ask if we are so wise now.
When all is not well words dare not fail
to be the questions that answer all
the world will ask of doubt and shame.
Our will is articulate
in finding the meaning
of a balance of possibilities.
We wince in the raw air of winter,
considering how we might measure
a scar, a snare, a nonsense
where once there was reason.
The echo may sound careworn
in its reaches of feeling.
Measure restores the love of mercy.

Eadweard Muybridge Time 11-15

by Christopher Barnes

MANUS

Needlework in   Letterpress Ps   Smithereened glass.
Scalp. Gore   And Qs.   Footprints muck-up
On P.E. kit.   Stockpiled bales.   Sill.

LUKE

Lady Penelope   Viscous feed   Suitcase vacuumed.
Bobs arm.   Into jardinière.   Passport thumbed.
Sputnik chair   Gust through
Rustles.   Unfastened sash.

HERBERT

Heroism inked.   Pyramid of   Foozled call.
Vainglory in.   Tins. Customer   Sudoku puzzle.
Speech bubbles.   Directions.

ALBERTINE

Poodle confident,   Stout froth   Piano charges
Foregrounding ignited   Dribbles. Pork   At Monteverdi. Basso
Hoop. Rope   Scratchings breathe.   Hassles lungs.
Anticipates sequins.

SINCLAIR

Raffia weave.   Undertowing bass.   Bleach-mottled
Stubborn twine   Insteps withstand   Slippers. Gamboge
On nails.   The tide   Lino.
                     Of Soul.

The Minor Keys
by David de Young

I got wine drunk in the Holiday Inn Notre Dame
with a view of the Eiffel Tower
put on Brahms Symphony #1 in C Minor

and was back in my British History classroom
on an August night in 1982
on the second floor of Alumni Recitation Hall

working out ways to include
English Beat and Gang of Four lyrics
in my poly sci and econ finals

blasting the Sir Georg Solti 1979 recordings
with the Chicago Symphony Orchestra
on my Sony Walkman and portable speakers

bought for me by a girl who'd sympathized
I'd fallen in love with her
O the power of the minor keys

reaching across the years There were times
I would have traded Brahms's four symphonies
for Beethoven's nine and skipped away

happy and that was one of them
So many things were clear to me then
before the wine and Paris and the years

Fourteen by Ten (a Sowhynot)
by Ken Gosse

So why not use a classic form but bend the rules from norm,
like this, which borrows artistry of classic sonnetry
but switches 'round the flowing sound which sonnets will perform,
whose shards came down from greater bards whose words had been set free?

Should this be done? Would anyone of sanity agree
to mock such grace and then to place them kiltered, at a slant?
Their numbered lines and their confines of syllables would be
laid on their side. Can it abide when others say, "You can't!"?

Yet here it's done—but has it won or lost the heart of those
who claim to own forms set in stone as this comes to its close?

Buying a Leather Jacket in Fez
by John Delaney

Stone vats of colored dyes and white liquids.
Hides of cows, sheep, goats, and camels.
The eager salesman explained the process,
how hides need to soak for two or three days
among cow urine and pigeon feces
to clean and soften the skins for the dyes,
natural colorants like indigo
and henna and poppy. Then they are dried
in the sun. Craftsmen create the products
by hand—slippers and handbags and jackets—
using methods from the Middle Ages.

Of course, their products were special, he said.
To prove the point, he lit a little flame
and held it up against the supple leather
that surprisingly seemed flame retardant.
Which leads me to think there's no reason why
I can't safely stride through raindrops and fire.

Well, at least it should keep me warm and dry.

Fez (or Fes), the second largest city in Morocco, has been called the "Athens of Africa" and is considered the spiritual and cultural capital of the country.

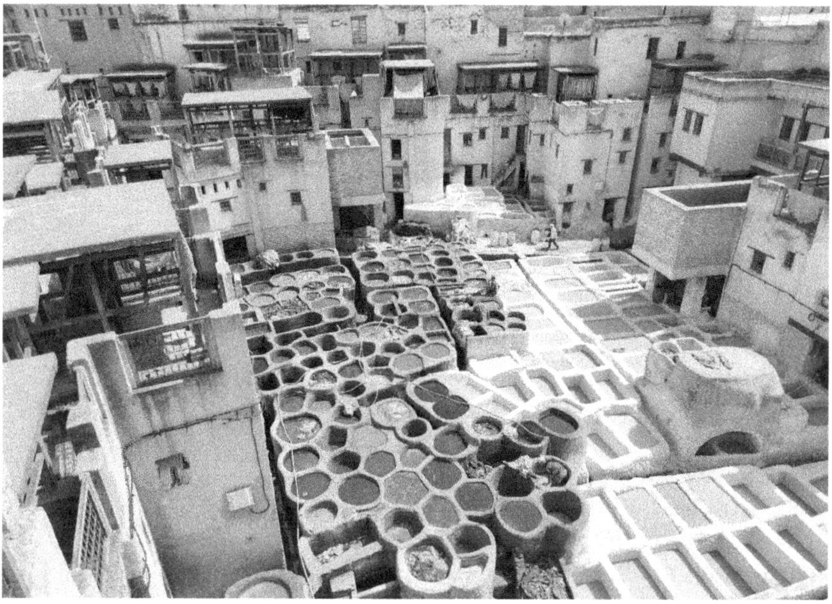

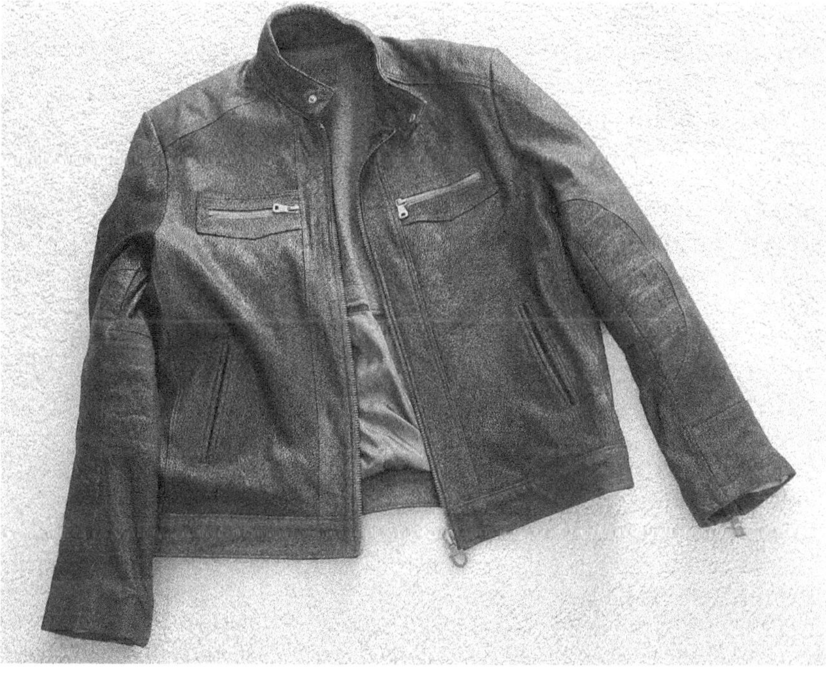

A Doorway
by Marianne Taylor

Your gaze speaks
to my own deep ice
Not sentiment
more elemental
unsettling

Perhaps we met
in a sculptor's studio
He shaped my shoulders, neck
labored on my breasts
You watched
enigma eyes inset
beard unchiseled

How long did we stare?
Were we modeled
for common patrons
but cast as amorous
gods, to please--
my arms, Aphrodite
Ares, your brow

Surely we rested
in velvet dirt, your chest
against my spine
hefting a mountain
upon us. These
alchemies hardened
deep secrets in our veins

yet stone's justness
yields no clues
to our knowing
It's old, cold,
stoically silent
mirrored in your

silence, my own set
mouth, the empty
arch of a doorway

Les Misérables Reviewed
by Lynette Esposito

It is an old story of disfunction.
While I see the beauty of a crow
that has an ugly voice
but a wonderful wing spread
undulating shadows in the sky,
controlling the sun's light
falling to earth,
its feathers holding the air,
you see only a bird.

Dancing Cherubs, Hotel de la Marine, Paris 1°

by Roger Camp

Bios

CHRISTOPHER BARNES
In 1998 Christopher Barnes won a Northern Arts writers award. In July 2000 he read at Waterstones bookshop to promote the anthology 'Titles Are Bitches'. Christmas 2001 he debuted at Newcastle's famous Morden Tower doing a reading of poems. Each year he read for Proudwords lesbian and gay writing festival and partook in workshops. 2005 saw the publication of his collection LOVEBITES published by Chanticleer Press, 6/1 Jamaica Mews, Edinburgh.
On Saturday 16Th August 2003 he read at the Edinburgh Festival as a Per Verse.
Christmas 2001 The Northern Cultural Skills Partnership sponsored him to be mentored by Andy Croft in conjunction with New Writing North. He made a radio programme for Web FM community radio about his writing group. October-November 2005, he entered a poem/visual image into the art exhibition The Art Cafe Project, his piece Post-Mark was shown in Betty's Newcastle. This event was sponsored by Pride On The Tyne. He made a digital film with artists Kate Sweeney and Julie Ballands at a film making workshop called Out Of The Picture which was shown at the festival party for Proudwords, it contains his poem The Old Heave-Ho. He worked on a collaborative art and literature project called How Gay Are Your Genes, facilitated by Lisa Mathews (poet) which exhibited at The Hatton Gallery, Newcastle University, including a film piece by the artist Predrag Pajdic in which he read his poem On Brenkley St. The event was funded by The Policy, Ethics and Life Sciences Research Institute, Bio-science Centre at Newcastle's Centre for Life. He was involved in the Five Arts Cities poetry postcard event which exhibited at The Seven Stories children's literature building. In May he had 2006 a solo art/poetry exhibition at The People's Theatre.

SIMONE BOUCHEY
Simone Bouchey writes (occasionally), reads (much more frequently) and yaps (constantly). She is endlessly curious about nearly everything, which has led her to teaching and learning across the globe. Her occasional writing and opinions on reading (from intellectual texts to alien smut) can be found on Substack.

ROGER CAMP
Roger Camp is the author of three photography books including the award

winning *Butterflies in Flight*, Thames & Hudson, 2002 and *Heat*, Charta, Milano, 2008. His work has appeared in numerous journals including *The New England Review*, *Witness* and the *New York Quarterly*. Represented by the Robin Rice Gallery, NYC, more of his work may be seen on Luminous-Lint.com.

MICKEY COLLINS
Mickey ~~rights wrongs~~. Mickey ~~wrongs rites~~. Mickey writes words, sometimes wrong words but he tries to get it write.

JOHN DELANEY
After retiring as curator of historic maps at Princeton University Library, I moved out to Port Townsend, WA, and have traveled widely, preferring remote, natural settings. Since that transition, I've published *Waypoints* (2017), a collection of place poems, *Twenty Questions* (2019), a chapbook, *Delicate Arch* (2022), poems and photographs of national parks and monuments, and *Galápagos* (2023), a collaborative chapbook of my son Andrew's photographs and my poems.

DAVID DE YOUNG
David de Young holds an MFA from NYU's Creative Writing program and is the proprietor of a small independent publisher, Nordic Moon Press. He lives in Finland with his wife and three children. In addition to poetry and short fiction, he writes regular essays about anything that strikes his fancy on his Substack, "Why This? Why Now?"

LYNETTE ESPOSITO
Lynette G. Esposito, MA Rutgers, has been published in *Poetry Quarterly*, *North of Oxford*, *Twin Decades*, *Remembered Arts*, *Reader's Digest*, *US1*, and others. She was married to Attilio Esposito and lives with eight rescued muses in Southern New Jersey.

ROBERT EVERSMANN
Robert Eversmann works for *Deep Overstock*.

KATE FALVEY
Kate Falvey's work has been published in many journals and anthologies including previous issues of *Deep Overstock*; in a full-length collection, *The Language of Little Girls* (David Robert Books); and in two chapbooks, *What the Sea Washes Up* (Dancing Girl Press) and *Morning Constitutional in Sunhat and Bolero* (Green Fuse Poetic Arts). She co-founded (with Monique Ferrell) and for ten years edited the *2 Bridges Review*, published through City

Tech (City University of New York) where she teaches, and is an associate editor for the *Bellevue Literary Review*.

Ken Gosse

Ken Gosse prefers writing short, rhymed verse with traditional meter and generally full of humor. First published in *The First Literary Review–East* in November 2016, since then in *Pure Slush, Lothlorien Poetry Journal, Academy of the Heart and Mind*, and others. Raised in the Chicago suburbs, now retired, he and his wife have lived in Mesa, AZ, over twenty years, usually rescue cats and dogs underfoot.

Michael Loyd Gray

My stories have appeared in Alligator Juniper, Arkansas Review, I-70 Review, Litro Magazine, Adelaide Literary Magazine, FictionWeek, New Plains Journal. Westchester Review, Flashpoint!, Black River Syllabary, Verdad, Palooka, Hektoen International, Potomac Review, Home Planet News, SORTES, The Zodiac Review, Literary Heist, Evening Street Press & Review, Two Thirds North, JONAH Magazine, Press Pause, El Portal, Shark Reef, Cholla Needles, The Waiting Room, Burningword Literary Journal, Your Impossible Voice, Litbop, Flare Journal, Fictional Café, Deep Wild, Wrath Bearing Tree, and Johnny America.

I'm the author of six published novels. My novel The Armageddon Two-Step, winner of a Book Excellence Award, was released in December 2019. My novel Well Deserved won the 2008 Sol Books Prose Series Prize and my novel Not Famous Anymore garnered a support grant from the Elizabeth George Foundation in 2009. My novel Exile on Kalamazoo Street was released in 2013 and I have co-authored the stage version. My novel The Canary, which reveals the final days of Amelia Earhart, was released in 2011. King Biscuit, my Young Adult novel, was released in 2012. I am the winner of the 2005 Alligator Juniper Fiction Prize and 2005 The Writers Place Award for Fiction.

I earned a MFA in English in 1996 from Western Michigan University, where I was a Phi Kappa Phi National Honor Society scholar (3.93 GPA). I was also a fiction editor for Third Coast, the WMU literary magazine. At WMU, I studied with MacArthur Fellow Stuart Dybek, Writer in Residence at Northwestern University, and John Smolens, former head of the MFA program at Northern Michigan University. I earned a bachelor's degree from the University of Illinois, where I studied with Flannery O'Connor Award winner Daniel Curley. For ten years, I was a staff writer for newspapers in Arizona and Illinois.

Heather Hambley

Heather is a Latin teacher turned translator. She has a BA in Classics from

Reed College, where she developed a passion for prose composition and mythological women. She lives in Central Oregon with her husband Andy and their senior poodle Mo. She loves watching scary movies and curates feel-good horror sets at happyspookies.substack.com.

Geoffrey Heptonstall

Geoffrey Heptonstall has worked as a bookseller , managing the Art section of Borders in Cambridge, England. Before that he took charge of French manuscripts for an independent academic publisher in Cambridge. His fourth collection of poetry, *A Whispering*, was published by Cyberwit June 2023. His first collection, *The Rites of Paradise*, received critical acclaim when first published in 2020. *Sappho's Moon* and *The Wicken Bird* followed. A novel, *Heaven's Invention*, was published by Black Wolf in 2016. *The Queen of Alsatia*, a novella, was published in Pennsylvania Literary Journal in 2023. A number of plays and monologues have been staged and/or published. He is also a prolific short fiction writer, essayist and reviewer.

RJ Equality Ingram

RJ Equality Ingram works as a used bookseller for Goodwill Industries of the Collumbia Willamette. Their first collection of poetry *The Autobiography of Nancy Drew* is forthcoming from White Stag Publishing in early 2024. RJ received their MFA in creative writing from Saint Mary's College of California with concentrations in poetry & creative nonfiction. More work can be found in *Phoebe Journal*, *Miniskirt Magazine* & *Citron Review* among others. RJ's cat Brenda lost a leg designing her memory palace.

Aletha Irby

My name is Aletha Irby and I have been writing poetry for over fifty years. My personal library includes books of poetry, mysteries, ghost stories, novels, and histories. My work has been published in *Main Street Rag*, *Lady Blue Literary Arts Journal*, *VOLT*, *Shot Glass Journal*, *Palo Alto Review*, *Tiny Lights Online*, and many other journals. I am very grateful to have been granted this time, on this planet, to spend with the English language.

Ivy Jong

Ivy Jong (she/they) is a queer writer focused on Classics and Greek myth. She is a bookseller at Powell's City of Books in Portland, Oregon.

Miles Kenny

Miles Kenny is a writer and lapsed historian. He works at Rose City Book Pub in Northeast Portland, OR, where he serves used books alongside food and drink. He spends much of his time thinking about stuff and a little bit of it writing stuff down.

James B. Nicola
James B. Nicola is a returning contributor. The latest three of his eight full-length poetry collections are *Fires of Heaven: Poems of Faith and Sense*, *Turns & Twists*, and *Natural Tendencies* (just out). His nonfiction book *Playing the Audience* won a *Choice* magazine award. He has received a Dana Literary Award, two *Willow Review* awards, *Storyteller's* People's Choice magazine award, one Best of Net, one Rhysling, and ten Pushcart nominations—for which he feels both stunned and grateful. A graduate of Yale, James hosts the Writers' Round Table at his library branch in Manhattan: walk-ins are always welcome.

Timothy Arliss Obrien
Timothy Arliss OBrien (he/they) is an interdisciplinary artist in music composition, writing, and visual art. He has premiered music from opera to film scores to electronic ambient projects. He has published several books of poetry, (*The Queer Revolt, The Art of Learning to Fly*, & *Happy LGBTQ Wrath Month*), and is a poetry editor for *Deep Overstock*, a judge for Reedsy Prompts, and a poetry reader for *Okay Donkey*. He also founded the podcast & small press publishing house, The Poet Heroic, and the digital magic space The Healers Coven. He also showcases his psychedelic makeup skills as the phenomenal drag queen Tabitha Acidz.
Check out more at his website: www.timothyarlissobrien.com

Craig Sautter
R. Craig Sautter is author, coauthor, editor of 11 books, including two of poetry: *Expresslanes Through The Inevitable City* and *The Sound of One Hand Typing*. His short stories have appeared in *Deep Overstock*, the *Chicago Quarterly Review, Evening Street Review, Catamaran, Neon Garden*.

Janis Lee Scott
Janis Lee Scott is an author from the San Joaquin Valley. She now lives in Oregon, writing and painting cows and lighthouses. She is a writer, a mother, a grandmother, and a volunteer. She is the official album artist for up-and-coming country and western star Reverend Shane.

Jihye Shin
Jihye Shin is a Korean-American poet and bookseller based in Florida.

Marianne Taylor
Marianne Taylor is a bookseller at Powell's on Burnside where she manages the sales floor in the Blue, Gold, and Green rooms. In a previous life she taught literature and creative writing at a Midwestern college, and her poetry has been published widely in national journals and anthologies. She once

served as Poet Laureate of her former small town, but for the past three years she's been trying to find her way around Portland.

Z.B. Wagman

Z.B. Wagman is an editor for the *Deep Overstock Literary Journal* and a co-host of the Deep Overstock Fiction podcast. When not writing or editing he can be found behind the desk at the Beaverton City Library, where he finds much inspiration.

Nicholas Yandell

Nicholas Yandell is a composer, who sometimes creates with words instead of sound. In those cases, he usually ends up with fiction and occasionally poetry. He also paints and draws, and often all these activities become combined, because they're really not all that different from each other, and it's all just art right?

When not working on creative projects, Nick works as a bookseller at Powell's Books in Portland, Oregon, where he enjoys being surrounded by a wealth of knowledge, as well as working and interacting with creatively stimulating people. He has a website where he displays his creations; it's nicholasyandell.com. Check it out!

All rights to the works contained in this journal belong to their respective authors. Any ideas or beliefs presented by these authors do not necessarily reflect the ideas or beliefs held by Deep Overstock's *editors.*